FR

OF

MIND

~ A DARK CORNER NOVEL ~

by

DAVID W. ADAMS

Also available in this series:

The Dark Corner

Return to the Dark Corner

Wealdstone

Resurrection

Wealdstone : Crossroads

FRAME OF MIND

For

Chantel, Iona, Emma, Sammie
and Emily,

For

Robyn and Josh,

And everybody else who
supported me and encouraged
me on my journey into the big
wide world.

Without you guys, this book
would not be possible.

And so, it is for you all.

CONTENT WARNING

Please be aware, that this is the darkest story so far in the Dark Corner Literary Universe, and as such I have decided for the first time, to include trigger warnings for some of the content. Please take note of these and proceed with caution if any of the following may cause you discomfort.

- **Mental Illness**
- **Blade related injuries**
- **Suicide**
- **Decapitation**
- **Mutilation**
- **Graphic description of injuries**
- **Institutionalised abuse**
- **Domestic Abuse**
- **Physical Assault**
- **Prolonged/Forced Captivity**
- **Hallucinations**
- **Unreality**
- **Experimental Drug Use**

Again, I urge you to continue with extreme caution and take breaks if you feel they are necessary. Here we go...

PROLOGUE

They say when your mind begins to unravel, you can almost feel the threads parting from the ball of string. The neurons and impulses grasp at the strands desperately trying to keep your mind whole, but it isn't enough. Before long, the things which make a person have dissipated, along with any resemblance to sanity.

This institution was no different. Sanity had long escaped its walls. Even the staff here were no longer entirely human. A long and bloody history, folded in with corruption, assault, manipulation and horror had created a forcefield of fear around the perimeter of the building. The general consensus was that if you entered Moriarty Hospital, you were never coming out.

Local people sometimes commented on the irony of naming a building after a wildly intelligent fictitious villain, but mostly they only spoke of whispers and rumours surrounding those inside. This was the largest sanitorium in the state and had been around far longer than the likes of nearby Trinity Bay.

Times however, despite how it may seem, do not change. Today was an example of this, as it was time for the annual inspection.

Previous visits had generated concern amongst professionals and directors, regarding the falling figures of those rehabilitated. Moriarty had over a thousand inmates, and three hundred full time staff and doctors. The expense of running all of that was beginning to be questioned as the funds weren't having the desired effect.

As Doctor Christian Verne led the contingent down the corridor of what had been dubbed by some of the staff as Cell Block D, he felt a distinct uneasiness. The sound of scribbling on paper covered clipboards set his teeth on edge. Usually, they started with the mild patients, cases of identity disorder under light medication, those who felt a danger to themselves rather than the public. But on this occasion, the group had demanded to be taken to the most desperate section of the hospital.

So far, the comments had been kept to a minimum, but there had been a shift in positions at boardroom level, and that brought with it a feel of an audit. Christian did not care for audits.

"Sir, may I ask when was the last time this area was refurbished?"

The question came as a surprise to Christian, who stopped in his tracks and turned back to face the woman who had posed the question.

"I'm sorry?" he asked, unsure he had heard correctly.

The woman looked at a colleague, who shrugged his shoulders, before repeating her question.

"I asked how recently the place was refurbished."

Christian wanted to laugh out loud, which was another sensation which caught him off guard. He did however, let out a slight sarcastic snort. One which the woman caught.

"Refurbished? Well… never. This is exactly as the hospital appeared when it reopened at the dawn of the twentieth century."

The woman seemed shocked, and hurriedly scribbled that down. The reopening in question had been after a fire in the admissions building spread to one of the wings and claimed the lives of seventy-five patients. That section of the hospital was never rebuilt, and instead relandscaped into a garden area.

Another of the group piped up next.

"So are you saying that these people have lived in this squalor for their entire duration?"

That comment irked Christian massively.

"These patients do not live in squalor, Mr. Francis. These cell… rooms, are cleaned to the highest standard, taking every precautionary measure of safety and security possible. Do not let a few chips of paint fool your brain into thinking otherwise."

Another flurry of scribbled notes, and Christian rolled his eyes back into his head, and let out an unimpressed sigh. The temperature had dropped somewhat in the afternoon, and his breath expanded into mist, before dissipating. The tour continued to move forwards, and Christian began his usual rollcall for the money brigade.

"These four rooms on the left contain the victims of the events at the Maximum Velocity megastore in Trinity Bay. Three security guards and a young woman who claimed to have been possessed by a demon that caused her to kill her friends."

The first interruption.

"Why exactly were the guards affected? They weren't there were they?"

Clearly, these people didn't watch the news. Either that, or they had no understanding of the human psyche.

"Mr Francis, if you had to go into a building that contained the mutilated bodies of several teenagers, a basement with satanic markings and yet another body, and be interrogated as to why your security system failed, then I'm pretty sure your mind would begin to unravel also. May we continue?"

Pen met paper once more.

"The young woman in question has had her time with us increased due to this so called demon returning and causing her to slit the throat of one of our security guards. All attempts at medicating the symptoms have so far failed, and we are unable to get a coherent sentence out of her."

Christian turned a corner into a darker corridor, away from the edge of the building which contained no windows. The air was colder still here, and several of the lights above them flickered in and out of illumination.

"This is what we have dubbed the 'Wealdstone Wing'. In the last decade or so, we have admitted forty-three patients from that area, all alluding to some kind of supernatural occurrence. For the most part, we treat them with anti-hallucinogenic drugs, and regular counselling sessions, but for those locked away in this part of Moriarty, it is stronger methods that are required."

The original woman cleared her throat.

"Stronger methods?" she asked, sheepishly.

Christian looked over his shoulder, but did not turn around.

"Electro-shock, stronger medication. And some experimental methods which you'll find details of in your information packs."

The group continued through the hospital, with Christian sarcastically detailing the cases before them. Several with schizophrenia, one or two with extreme kinds of psychosis, and several who had committed incredibly violent acts, but had no recollection of doing so. Upon reaching the end of the corridor, Mr Francis noticed there was a singular room with a narrower door, set apart from the rest.

"Dr Verne, what is that room for in the corner?" he asked.

Christian turned an realised which door he was referring to.

"Maximum security. That room contains our most violent inmate. And I use the word inmate instead of patient, because if she weren't medically insane, she would be on death row right now."

Propelled by curiosity, Mr Francis and the others began to creep towards the door.

"I wouldn't do that if I were you," Christian warned, not moving towards the door with them.

But they did not listen. There was a small window in the centre of the door itself, but no light emerging from within. Mr Francis and the woman gazed through the glass, their faces almost pressed up against the cold metal surface of the door. The room was completely shrouded in darkness. No movement. No sound.

Mr Francis turned his head to look at Christian.

"I don't see anybody."

Christian giggled.

"No, but she can see you."

As Mr Francis turned his face back towards the glass, the contorted face of a woman threw itself at the glass window, shrieking in agony and her fists began pounding at the door. Mr Francis and the woman threw themselves back in fear, both landing on their backsides, much to Christian's delight. When they got back to their feet, the woman was gone.

"How many psychopaths like that do you have here, Verne?" demanded Mr Francis, now angry and embarrassed.

"Oh we have twenty-one murderers, sixteen rapists, a dozen or so paedophiles… but only one of her. She is unique."

The woman furiously scribbled down notes on the situation before storming down the corridor with the others. Mr Francis stopped one of them and pointed to the door.

"Take the room number down and the patients' name. I want to know more about her treatment."

"Yes, Mr Francis."

The younger assistant edged towards the door, speaking as he wrote down the requested details.

"Room number... 47. Patient name... Kristin Silverton."

ONE

Nine months ago

"Okay, so what do we have Chief?"

The smoke was still billowing up from the wreckage of the building despite it now being extinguished. The Fire Chief strolled over towards the detective and his partner.

"We got a goddamn mess, Frank. That's what we got."

Frank held his hands up. He had been having a fairly good day until the call came over the radio for all available units to attend the scene of a series of potential murders and arson. He'd even managed to stop by the new *Tim Hortons* on the way into the station that morning.

"Just the details, Miles. Cut the sarcastic shit. I'll get you a Banoffee French Vanilla latte later?"

The Chief's caffeine intake was dangerously low, so he nodded and removed his helmet.

"Got a report of a small fire at the back of the store about an hour ago. One unit arrived to find the whole place burning. That's when the shitstorm rained down. Four engines later, we discover the culprit, sat on the curb over there, rocking back and forth in a pool of blood that wasn't her own, cradling a knife."

The two of them turned to look over at a woman, no older than thirty-five with matted brown hair, and her clothes drenched in crimson. There was so much blood, there was no way to tell what colour her outfit was originally. She was currently cuffed to an ambulance trolley, and her legs held down by leather straps.

"She set the fire?" asked Frank.

Miles shook his head.

"She killed the people inside, and burnt the bodies. *That* is what caused the fire in the building."

Frank looked at the woman again, wrestling against the restraints, but no emotion on her face. He thought he vaguely recognised her though, and it troubled him.

"How do we know she killed them? You know, apart from the redecorating she's done on her outfit."

Miles turned slightly to his left and pointed at a young man, being comforted by paramedics around six feet away.

"We have a survivor. And he has phone footage. Says she strolled into the store, calm as you like, picked up a bag of Reeses Pieces, walked up to the counter, and then it was like her face changed. That's all I could get out of him."

Frank nodded, and sent his partner over to take a look at the apparent maniac on the gurney. He moved towards the young man, who was now sipping from a cup of water.

"Hey there."

The young man instantly flinched, and dropped his water. Frank held up his hands.

"Hey it's okay. I'm Detective Frank Short. Chief Hernandez tells me you saw the whole thing. Wanna tell me about it?"

The young man shook his head, and looked away. His eyes kept darting back and forth like his mind was trying to keep itself together. However, although he did not wish to speak about the events, he reached into his pocket and pulled out his phone. Handing it to Frank, his hands were shaking. He took the phone, which was open to a video file.

"Thank you," he nodded and walked over to the side of the neighbouring building away from the young man.

Frank tapped play on the video. It appeared to be of the man who had given it to him and a friend trying to see how much they could fit in a shopping cart without it falling out. Typical social media fodder. However, in the background, the woman now on the gurney behind him walked into shot, and the young man could be heard.

"Woah, that chick's hot."

The video did indeed show her walking up to the chocolate and placing it on the counter. She even smiled at the clerk. But then it turned violent. Her entire face changed, like she had left a room and someone else had walked in. It may have been his imagination, but he swore he saw a flash of purple in her eyes. Without hesitation, she reached up, grabbed the clerk's head and twisted violently to the side and up, snapping his neck. He fell to the floor in a heap, and the screams of the young man and his friend could be heard in the video.

"Run Sid! Chick's crazy!"

The woman snapped her head around, and lunged towards them, the camera shaking as they tried to run. As it panned round, it caught the woman straddling the young man's friend, who was now lying on the floor, and she was repeatedly punching him in the face. With each heavy blow, more and more of his features disappeared, the blood spraying against her own clothes and face.

It was at this point that she stopped, stood up to her full height and headed towards the store entrance. Another member of the public had come into the store, and before he could even survey what had happened, she was upon him. He resisted at first, attempting to draw a knife out of his jacket pocket, but she grabbed the instrument and used it to puncture his chest five times, before he dropped to the ground.

What happened next bemused Frank. The video had been horror filled almost from the start, but this was *unholy*. The woman dragged each body into a different position in the store, and moved her way towards the lighter fluid behind the counter. The young man filming was clearly still hiding, unable to move. The camera was still shaking, and his heavy laboured breath could be heard in the microphone.

As Frank watched the video, she poured the fluid onto each of the bodies in turn, before returning to them in sequence, and lighting a match tossing it onto the victims. She then moved directly in line with the camera and stopped, and it was like somebody switched on the light in an empty house. All recognition came back to her face, and as she looked around at what she had done, still clutching the knife of the third victim, she dropped to her knees and let out an earth shattering scream of absolute agony. There was no resemblance at all to the brutal emotionless killer of just moments before. As the flames grew around them, the young man took his chance and bolted past the woman who was now pulling furiously at her hair and out of the store. That's where the footage ended.

Frank lowered the phone and took several deep breaths. He looked up to see his partner walking towards him, holding what looked like a wallet.

"What's the verdict, Beth?" he asked.

His partner was clearly troubled, despite her not having seen the harrowing footage. Her southern drawl always managed to calm him down or ease his mind. His mother had been from the south, and she often reminded him of her despite her young age.

"I thought I recognised her, when we got here," Beth said, turning the wallet around to show Frank the ID. "It's Kristin Silverton."

Frank had been on duty in Wealdstone several years ago when the shopping district first opened. The place was an eyesore, and put a lot of good independent stores out of business, but he was only a uniform officer then, so kept his mouth shut, earned his wage, and went home.

"Last I heard, she'd gone AWOL. Her movie theatre manager reported her missing a few months ago, before withdrawing the report."

Beth nodded.

"I enquired with the precinct, and before she disappeared, she signed divorce papers from her wife Kathryn Silverton. Nobody had seen her since."

Frank handed the wallet back to his partner. He had heard about the rumours surrounding what had happened in Wealdstone. There had been too much noise to filter out the truth, but he often wondered if there were other forces at play with everything that was happening there. That sleepy little town had been in the news far too often for his liking.

"Did you manage to get any sense out of her?"

Beth shook her head.

"Kept mumbling something about pain, being unable to control it. Asked for help, and then passed out. They're taking her to Trinity Bay General. It's the nearest facility."

Frank scoffed.

"Trinity Bay is a wasteland. Remind me why you're transferring there?"

Beth raised her eyebrows.

"You know when Dad asks me for help, there's no turning him down. Although there was something about that place that just felt like home. When I visited Dad last year, he tried to flesh out his plan. I even managed to pop into Will's bar. That's where I saw Ms. Silverton. She was there with her former wife."

"Speaking of former love interests, I hear you'll be working with one of yours?"

Beth jabbed him in the arm.

"It's been a year since I found out about that, and I'm still not ready to talk about it. Besides, seems like we have our hands full here. This is absolutely gonna keep me busy for my last week."

The two of them shared a brief chuckle, before Frank returned to the case.

"Alright, I want a full statement, written or verbal from that young man as soon as he is able. I'll head to TBG and see what I can get from Ms. Silverton. From what I've seen in this video footage, she's a prime candidate for Moriarty."

Beth actively shuddered at the sound of that name. The hospital in question was notorious for containing the purest forms of evil and sadness. She had seen for herself the conditions inside when she was tasked with a patient escort a year ago. She had vowed never to set foot in there again.

As the ambulance disappeared round the corner of the street, she headed towards the second ambulance loading up the young man, and hopped inside. Frank meanwhile, headed back to their car.

"Hey Frank?"

The Fire Chief's voice echoed across the street.

"You'd better not forget my latte!"

Frank smiled and climbed into his car.

TWO

The gradual drip, drip, drip from the corroded pipe in the ceiling was the only sound, echoing around the empty shower room. The pace remained constant. Unaltered. The lights in here were bright and stark, revealing the true grime and decay of the building. The tiles were cracked and the grout between them was now blotched with black mould. The shower heads had long since rusted from their shiny reflective beginnings.

Kristin stood deathly still beneath her assigned shower head. Cold, naked, absent. Make no mistake, she was not unaware of her surroundings, but she was actively trying to anchor herself to a specific point in time in order to maintain some level of control over her thoughts. Her mind. Anything she could do to stop the ball of string from unravelling any further.

"Get a move on, 47. I ain't got all day."

The voice of the female security guard shattered both the almost silent air, but Kristin's concentration. Every time this occurred, her mind would begin replaying the picture show behind her eyes. One thousand lifetimes of pain and death and torture, all on repeat, the speed increasing with each playback. The phantom pains in every area she had been hurt in the Realm of Screams. Charging up her anger. Charging up her hatred. She became a beacon of violent electricity. And every time this happened, she unconsciously found herself an outlet.

"I said, hurry up!"

Another break in concentration, and Kristin visibly shuddered.

"For fuck's sake, 47. You want me to scrub you down? Because frankly I got better things to do!"

The voice of the female guard was now awakening the more recent painful memories.

Kathryn.

Jack.

Daniella.

Those names joined the symphony of agony. The imagery of her wife and Jack together. The imagery of Daniella discarding her like some sort of used comfort blanket. The realisation of the end of her marriage. And the replayed memory of her signing divorce papers.

"Right that's it."

The guard took four large strides forward, and shoved Kristin aside. With a sharp yank to the left, the tap brought the shower head to life. She grabbed Kristin on her already bruised arm, and dragged her under the water, grabbed a bar of soap, and slapped it hard into the centre of her chest. Kristin grabbed the soap, instinctively, and the guard backed off. As she retraced two of her strides towards the entrance to the shower block, the light above her buzzed and began to flicker. She paused and looked up.

Behind her, Kristin was increasing her grip on the bar of soap, which was now beginning to alter shape with the force. Again, the light buzzed and flickered. The guard withdrew her baton, and lifted it above her, tapping the casing surrounding the light. It stopped flickering.

"Hmm. That did it."

Satisfied with her apparent success at electrical repair work, she returned to the entrance, and span on her heels to look back at Kristin.

But she was gone.

"Oh shit."

The guard reached for her radio, and the usual beep as she depressed the button mingled with the sound of the still running water.

"Control, I may have a problem. Request backup to shower block 4, over."

Another beep.

"Control here, all received. Back up en route."

The officer returned her radio to its clip, and pulled her gun, laying it over her opposing wrist for added control. She cautiously stepped forward towards the shower. As she gazed down, the crushed bar of soap was lying in a puddle of water, foaming as the shower head pummelled it into the cracked tiles.

The lights above her all began to flicker and buzz, flashing intermittently in random sequence, creating pockets of darkness around the room. From behind her, she felt a sharp gust of air, and she span around, gun still raised.

Nothing.

"47? Where are you? I got back up coming."

Another gust of wind behind her to her right. Spinning around, she thought she caught sight of Kristin's naked behind disappearing into the next section of showers. She moved forward at a slightly accelerated pace, and turned the corner. But there was no sign. Then, her radio began to crackle on its own.

Of the thirty or so lights in the room, twenty of them blew out, one by one in a line approaching the guard. Her eyes grew wide, and she aimed her gun towards the ceiling targeting some unseen force.

And then they stopped.

Her breathing echoed around her, and she gradually managed to get it under control. But as she did so, she felt another breath behind her left ear. She span round as quickly as she could, but it was not fast enough. Kristin grabbed the side of her head with one hand, and slammed it into the tiled wall next to her. The guard's forehead split, and blood began to trickle down the side of her face. She attempted to raise her gun, but Kristin grabbed her other wrist, and twisted sharply, the sound of the bones cracking piercing the air, followed by a shriek from the guard.

The gun clattered to the floor, and Kristin slammed her face into the wall again. This time several tiles fell from the wall in pieces. A third strike, and her nose shattered, blood exploding from her face and spraying the tiles. The fourth and final time into the wall caused her hair to fall from its bun and become matted with the blood now pouring from her face. Kristin let go of her head, and she dropped to the floor. The guard was twitching on the floor, and gradually opened her left eye. Kristin looked down at her, and her head tilted slightly to the side. Her eyes looked like they were flashing with a small glint of violet light. The guard coughed and spluttered and tried to gain some traction on the wet tiles to push herself away with any remaining strength, but Kristin moved forward, slowly, wet hair clinging to her now blood splattered skin. She knelt down alongside the guard, and her fingers found a shard of tile. She grasped it, and with a speed not possible with most humans, thrust the piece of tile forward, and under the guards' chin and upwards.

As the life left her body, Kristin stood up once more, turned and walked around the corner back to her shower. The lights returned and a moment later, Kristin found herself blinking away a strange glow in her vision. She picked up the bar of soap and began washing herself as if nothing had happened. And then the memory of what had just happened fired into her subconscious like a bullet to the brain. Her face contorted into a vision of pure terror and as the other guards entered the room, she could hear the commotion as one found the body of her escort.

As she was tackled to the ground, her head ricocheted off the floor, and she slipped into a state of unconsciousness. As she did so, she glanced at the ceiling and she saw what looked like an oil slick moving across the ceiling towards the exit.

And then she fell into darkness.

THREE

The office of Dr Christian Verne was the most immaculate room in the entire facility. Certificates, and trophies lined the south wall. Achievements and accomplishments from medical awards, to golfing trophies and even a 'Man of the Year' award. It was accolades like this which gave the man somewhat of a God complex. He had begun to believe he was above the people he was surrounded with, and was now reaching the point where he believed his mere presence was enriching the lives of those around him, and that they should be grateful.

However, there was always something trying to set him back and tarnish his good name. And he was now sat opposite one of them.

"Ms. Silverton, do you realise what your actions this time have caused?"

"Booth."

Cristian was confused.

"I'm sorry?"

Kristin looked up with her eyes, but did not move her head.

"My name is Booth. Silverton was my married name. That's over now."

Trivial details. Certainly not something that would impact his treatment of the woman.

"You were admitted here under your married name, and so that is what you will be addressed as whilst you're a guest in my facility. Ms. Silverton."

As he repeated the name, he formed a wry smile in the corner of his mouth. Kristin was now doing everything in her power to suppress the images of pain and rage within her. Two guards flanked her on either side, with further three outside the office. Given her recent behaviour, it was a risk Christian thought necessary. While he appeared strong and resolute, he was a coward. After all, people like him had other people doing his dirty work.

"You were brought here, because it was believed you'd lost your mind. However, I must say that in that time, you have demonstrated to me that you are much more calculated in your movements. Three patients wounded, two killed. Four guards hospitalised and now one dead. Your movements seem too precise, too controlled for a simple member of the public. I think there are things you aren't telling me."

Kristin's head began to twitch slightly as she struggled to form her replies. The slideshow had started up again, and she was trying to leave the theatre of her mind.

"I've told you countless times, you simply choose to ignore me. You punish me. You torture me. If anything, whatever monster I've become should be more proof to you that my stories are true."

Christian stood up and walked over to a side table next to the window, and poured himself a cup of black coffee. He scooped three sugars into the liquid and stirred gently, tapping the spoon on the edge of the cup three times, his eyes moving to the side to try and catch Kristin's reaction. As he had hoped, the sound made her flinch. It was something he had noticed in their first encounter and deliberately used the technique every time since.

Returning to his desk, he took a large sip of the coffee, and placed the cup down on his desk before leaning back in his chair.

"Ms. Silverton, if I were to believe the stories of every inmate in here, I would have to accept so many different fantasies that I may myself have to be committed. I find it much more likely that you are a secret operative, placed here to undermine my practices. So I suggest you come clean."

Despite the war going on inside her head, Kristin was able to form a confused look on her face.

"You think I'm a what?"

Christian took another slurp of coffee.

"It's quite simple really. I have been threatened with closure for Moriarty for several years now. I suspected somebody may try and sneak in an undercover agent of some sort. After all, some of our methods are not yet… approved for use by the official boards and channels."

Kristin struggled against her restraints as she leaned forwards, the leather straps digging into her skin.

"You're such a fucking idiot. There is something in this hospital. Something dark. *I've seen it.*"

She whispered the last sentence, and Christian paused for a moment. He leaned forward as close to her as he dared, and whispered back.

"Do tell."

Kristin spoke through gritted teeth.

"What I've experienced… what I've done… it's created some kind of demon within me, I know that. But there's something here, amplifying it. I saw it in the showers last night. A black mass. There's a darkness here. An all consuming darkness. And it's getting stronger."

Christian never broke eye contact during every word Kristin said. When she was done, he leaned back once more, and placed his hands together at their fingertips in a triangular shape. For what seemed like an eternity, he said nothing, his eyes never leaving the face of the woman before him.

Part of him wanted to believe that she was genuinely afflicted with something. But recent events with the board and the concerted efforts to find evidence to close Moriarty for good had left him a very sceptical individual. A very cynical man. He leaned in once more, slightly closer this time. Enough for Kristin to feel his breath on her face.

"There is a darkness here, Ms Silverton. It surrounds you, and everyone you touch. I'm afraid we are going to have to take more... extreme measures to gain the truth from you."

He looked up at the guards and nodded his head. They moved forward in unison, and lifted both Kristin and the chair she was strapped to, and began to carry her out of the room.

"NO! YOU DON'T UNDERSTAND! IF YOU THINK I'M THE WORST THING IN HERE, YOU'RE WRONG!"

The door closed behind her, and Christian took another sip of his coffee. The taste seemed slightly more bitter, the liquid darker. These measures were not something he enjoyed, but he had worked too hard to establish his position, his reputation, for someone to try and undermine him. This was his kingdom, and nobody was going to take that from him.

FOUR

The cold, hard surface of her cell floor was a soothing sensation to her face as she was thrown back into her cell. The door slammed shut and the lock clicked into place behind her. Kristin had not yet fully recovered from the more extreme measures that Dr Verne had authorised. Although the room was bathed in darkness, she could see the streaks of fresh blood shining as they moved down her arms, and her fingertips felt the stickiness of her blood as it trickled onto the floor. Her face was now swollen, and her skin tingled from the higher doses of electroshock therapy she had just endured.

The only consolation she could take from the beating and the trauma of what she had just felt, was that it allowed her mind to move away from the usual bombardment of imagery. While she was undergoing pain in real time, the memories lay dormant. It was when she was not being hurt, that the real pain flourished.

She managed to push herself up against the nearest wall, and pull herself into a seated position. Catching her breath, she wiped a trickle of blood from the corner of her mouth. She did not cry. There were no more tears to give.

And then she felt it.

There were eyes on her. She could sense it. Just like she had done in the showers before she passed out. She saw nothing in the darkness, but she could *feel* it crawling over her skin. And then it spoke to her.

"Kristin."

She jolted at the sound of her name spoken in such a serpent like manner. Again, it spoke to her, but this time it whispered directly into her ear, and her hair moved slightly with the breath accompanying it.

"Kristin."

Kristin clenched her fists tightly, her long untrimmed fingernails digging into her palms, but she did not flinch.

"Who's there?" she asked, too terrified to move.

"Kristin."

This time, the voice came from the doorway, and the sound of the lock being turned, made her jump away from the wall. The huge metal door swung open, the hinges creaking as it did so. Kristin looked out into the hallway, but saw nobody. Every fibre in her already disturbed being told her not to leave that room, but the voice was hypnotic.

"Kristin… find me."

She found herself clambering to her feet, and almost on some kind of auto-pilot. She made her way to the door, and looked around. The hallway was empty, lights on minimum levels. She stepped out of her room, her bare feet sticking to the tiled floor. One of the lights at the end of the corridor began to flicker, just as it had done in the showers. Kristin looked up and saw the thing she had tried to warn Verne about earlier in the day.

A large black mass, constructed of long twisting strands of what looked like oil, clung to the ceiling near the light. She froze on the spot, and watched as it slowly began to move towards her. As it reached each light, they went dark, a loud clunking noise echoing along the hallway as it did so. A sharp pain fired into Kristin's temple, causing her to wince and drop to the floor. She squeezed the sides of her head, her eyes clenched shut, the echoing of the lights shutting off getting louder as whatever it was got closer and closer.

Suddenly, the pain was gone, the noise stopped, and Kristin opened her eyes. She was still on the floor of her cell, door locked, surrounded in darkness and silence.

Her breathing was rapid and heavy, and her heart was pounding. She searched in the darkness for answers or signs of movement, but found nothing. And then the theatre show returned to the screen in her mind, and her eyes glowed a soft violet and she once more descended into madness.

As Kristin pounded on her door with her fists, the sounds echoed down the empty silent corridor, all night long.

FIVE

The next morning, Kristin awoke in her room, lying on the floor, and as she glanced up, she saw in the limited daylight, smeared blood leading from the bulletproof glass window, all the way down to the floor. It traced its way along the cold tiles until it reached the place where she was lying. Raising her hands in front of her, she could see her fingernails were broken, and her fists were bloody and bruised.

But what was really confusing her, was the fact that she was still here. There was no clock inside her room, but it was very rare for her not to be dragged off down the corridor at the crack of dawn for some kind of treatment. Pushing away her condition for a moment, she pulled herself along to the nearest wall, dragging her feet, and lifted herself up. Gradually, she staggered over to the little window in the door, and peered through.

Chaos.

Although she was at the end of the corridor, the reflective metal surface on the end wall allowed her to see what was going on outside. At least ten security guards lined either side of the hallway, and the irritated figure of Dr Christian Verne stood between them in front of one of the other cell doors. She squinted, trying to focus and saw what looked like a hospital gurney being wheeled out of the room in question. But there was no patient on it.

It carried a black body bag.

Kristin gasped out loud, and moved her hand to her face. She knew who that room had belonged to. It had been where Nat was placed just before she had arrived. They had only had a couple of conversations during their time together, usually due to one or both of them slipping into a frenzy, but Nat had told her how she had become possessed by some kind of malevolent force in Trinity Bay, and was convinced she had killed at least four of her friends before the entity abandoned her. It had made Kristin feel more comfortable in a way. There was some kinship between them that made her feel like she wasn't alone.

In response, Nat had shown great interest in her tale for the same reasons. Although she had confessed there was no way she could feel what it must have been like to go through such torture and agony, she too felt comforted by the fact that Kristin had suffered at the hands of the paranormal.

Those brief memories were soon obliterated though, when Kristin realised that it had been next to Nat's room, where the mysterious black entity had stopped the previous night. She never knew for certain whether these experiences were real or part of the madness now dominating her mind, but with this one, she had the answer.

It had all been real.

Then the panic began to set in. What was this evil entity, and where did it come from? Why did she feel stronger in its presence? Was it amplifying her craziness, or drawing power from it somehow? And why was it calling to her? Whichever way she tried to analyse it, she couldn't come up with the answer.

Her mind was unravelling more and more each day, and she wasn't sure how much longer she could hold it together. She had regained some degree of control over the explosions of pain, and anger, but it was becoming more and more difficult.

From out of nowhere, Kristin's mind shifted to the face of her former wife. Her eyes were open and continuing to look through the doorway at the metal surface beyond, but displayed on that surface, was the face of Kathryn Silverton. Previously, of course, Kathryn's face would have been a beacon of hope and a sign for joy. But after the events at Crossroads, her joy had been soured, and the image caused a surge in anger.

Kristin felt the rage begin to build within her, and the carousel of images started up once again. A tiny piece of her tried to force the imagery back down to the darkened depths from which it came, but she was failing. Her eyes bolted open, and there was a small flicker of violet in them, before she let out a bloodcurdling roar and began once again hammering at the door.

From down the corridor, the security guards leapt into action and flew in her direction, Dr Christian along with them, although hanging at the back of the pack. To their amazement, they saw the steel door take such a hit from inside, that a fist mark appeared on the *outside*. All of them stopped, unsure of what to do next. None of their training had prepared them for that level of strength. Another hit, another exterior dent in the metalwork.

"What are you waiting for? Go!"

Christian was not prepared to wait and see how this was going to pan out. If anything, he was now more convinced that Kristin was on some kind of steroids, perhaps as part of the black ops training he suspected. One way or another, he needed to get to the root of the truth. Step one, would be taking her down.

The guards continued to advance, and as they reached the point of the corridor that only contained Kristin's room, the hammering stopped, and all went quiet. They stopped once more, Christian cowering behind them.

BANG!

The entire door flew from its hinges, and launched across the hallway, smashing into the opposing wall, and clattering down to the ground, smashing dozens of tiles with its extreme weight. Only superhuman strength could have done something like that. They all watched on as Kristin slowly emerged from her room, walking straight until she was in the dead centre of the hallway.

She turned slowly, still looking down at the floor. Above her, the lights began to flicker as they had done the previous two nights.

Christian's heart was now getting ready to leap out of his chest, but the worst was not yet over. As he prepared to give the order to advance once more, he glanced up at the ceiling above Kristin, and to his horror, saw what he could only describe as an oil slick.

The black, glossy substance twisted and contorted above her, strands moving outward like tentacles, seemingly dragging the rest of it along. He tried to call out, but the scream stuck in his throat. The first flickering light blew out with such force, glass cascaded down over the guards. As they cowered to shield themselves, Kristin rushed forward, leaping into the air and wrapping her legs around the first male guard's head, twisting violently to the side, and snapping his neck. As she slid down, one of the female guards attempting to strike her with a baton, but Kristin grabbed it, yanked it away, and shoved it, wide end first directly into her mouth with such force, her jaw bones crunched, and the slightly pointed handle of the instrument erupted from the back of her throat.

"Take her OUT!" came the screams of the head security guard.

Christian was frozen to the spot, still fixated on whatever creature was slowly moving towards him. Another light exploded sending more glass down to the ground as Kristin continued to evade capture. She moved as though trained by the SAS, sliding beneath the legs of a third guard, and grabbing his left ankle, twisting violently until it snapped. As he collapsed to the floor in a heap, she straddled him and began pummelling his face from left to right until it no longer resembled its previous form.

Blood was now everywhere. Kristin's shirt and trousers were now stained crimson, her face a Jackson Pollock exhibit of red splatter patterns. The white tiles of the floor were also now slick with red. Two guards grabbed an arm each, while a third struck Kristin in the back with the butt of his gun. It was enough to cause Kristin to react slightly, but she continued to wrestle against her captors. Her left arm grabbed the bunch of cell keys from the waistband of the guard on her right arm, and she twisted around and jabbed a key directly into his eye socket. His eye popped like a balloon, and blood and optic fluid burst forward. He immediately lost his grip and flew to the ground grasping at his face, his screams echoing not only down the corridor, but throughout the hospital.

Another squad of security flew around the corner, and pushed past Christian, who was still staring at the black mass. They lined up blocking off the corridor, and all five of them opened fire on Kristin, a hail of rubber bullets striking her all over her body. She dropped to the floor, but a second wave of bullets struck her, knocking her onto her back. The assault had the desired effect. Kristin's mind began to become her own again, and as she came back to the realisation of where she was, she rolled and threw herself onto all fours, and let out a deafening scream of agony.

The only remaining guard from the original detachment approached her, and as she looked up at her, the guard brought her boot up to Kristin's face and slammed it down hard. Kristin's unconscious body collapsed back to the floor.

Christian watched as the creature on the ceiling began to slowly retreat. He blinked away a bead of sweat and when he opened his eyes again, the mass was gone. He looked down and saw the aftermath of Kristin's attack. Four guards dead. One standing over Kristin, delivering a few extra kicks to the abdomen to make sure she was indeed out cold, and a firing squad lining his hallway. It took him a few moments to gather his voice again.

"Dr, orders?" asked the guard standing over Kristin.

Christian cleared his throat.

"Tranquilise her, and have her taken down to the Basement Level. I think it's time we saw exactly what is in her head."

SIX

1 YEAR EARLIER

"Is there anything else I can help you with, my dear?" asked the Post Office clerk.

Kristin looked down at the papers she now held in her hand, and a shot of sadness flew through her. But the Post Office was not the place to cry, so she stuffed the papers into her jacket pocket, and smiled back at the clerk.

"No, that's great thank you. Thank you for your time."

She turned to leave, but the elderly clerk took the thanks as an excuse to continue a complaint she'd obviously started with a previous customer.

"No problem. Busier than ever now we're having to double as a budget lawyer administration. Never been so snowed under. I was only telling Sylvia this morning, how its not right just because the law office downtown isn't back up and running yet, doesn't mean we should be dishing out legal papers. I mean we haven't been trained to…"

Kristin held up her hand. She did not have the time or the mental ability to focus on such nonsense.

"I'm sorry, I really have to go. Thanks again."

The clerk continued speaking in the background, despite nobody else being there, but Kristin pushed the door and walked out into the street. The sun felt more and more intense with every hour. Her mind continued to swim with thoughts of the battle she had just been through.

It may not have been her first encounter with a powerful being, but she was determined that it would be her last. As she walked up the long driveway towards the house that her and Kathryn had shared, each step felt heavier than the last. She knew that it was over. And something had happened to her.

The experience of being sent to the Realm of Screams had clearly altered her mind. She could feel things beginning to take over that were so painful, her stomach began to churn. But it wasn't the mental aspect she was taken aback by. Something in her very DNA felt like it was changing.

Her muscles in the last hour had begun to tense and expand on their own. Her breathing had become more rapid, even in the few moments she had been at rest. Whatever was happening to her, she had to get away from Wealdstone and quick. The happiness and acceptance she had felt about her and Kathryn's mutual break up before the conflict, had now turned to anger and resentment.

She entered the house, and placed the divorce papers on the table, before going upstairs and grabbing a large duffel bag. She stuffed a selection of clothes, toiletries and underwear into the bag, and zipped it up, before slinging it over her shoulder and heading back down the stairs.

She spotted a pen on the floor near the mail table, and picked it up. She noticed there was a letter on the floor behind the table, that seemed different. The envelope was yellowed and the address seemed like it had been written by a calligrapher. Noise outside the front door distracted her, and she decided to pick up the pace. Ignoring the envelope, she grabbed the pen, and walked over to the papers. She signed her name in the relevant places, and placed the pen down next to them. Tears formed in her eyes, but she wiped them away, took a deep breath, and walked out of the house closing the door behind her. Reaching into a pocket, she pulled out two sets of keys. The first, the house keys, she posted back through the letterbox. The second belonged to her pet project.

Kristin walked around to the garages, and lifted the first door up. Inside was a musty smell, and dust rained from above. Although the house was only a couple of years old, the work Kristin had done on restoring what was in here had meant a lot of sawdust and plastic particles were present.

She reached down, grabbed a corner of the large dust sheet and yanked it away. Where the old dirty sheet had been, now sat a bright cherry red Ford Mustang. The chrome trim and grill shone in the glint of the evening sunlight, and Kristin saw her reflection clearly in the bodywork. She popped the trunk and threw her bag inside, slamming it down afterwards.

As she eased herself into the seat, and closed the door, she closed her eyes and inhaled the scent. Nineteen-sixties leather. Her favourite smell in the whole world. Kathryn had never been entirely enthusiastic about her taking a mechanics course with everything going on between them, but she had persevered and now, the car was here when nobody else remained.

She slipped the key into the ignition, turned it and the engine roared into life. Kristin put the car into drive and slammed her foot down on the gas pedal. The car lurched forward and out of the garage. Before too much longer, Kristin was flying down the interstate, engine humming in the background.

After a couple of hours driving, she realised that she had not planned a destination. Her desire to escape Wealdstone had overtaken everything else. Seeing a sign for a town called Wellsfield, she pulled off the main road, and drove the ten miles to the town limits. She looked out of the windows as she drove slowly down what appeared to be the main street.

"Not a bad little place," she said aloud to herself. "Definitely somewhere I could eat."

She pulled into the nearest parking space, got out, topped up the meter and headed over the road to what looked like a fifties era diner. The generic bell over the door chimed, and immediately, a waitress appeared at the counter with a pot of coffee.

"What can I get you, honey?" she asked.

Kristin slid onto a stool and placed her arms on the counter.

"I'll take a black coffee, double sweet, and whatever you have in the way of pie, please."

The woman nodded, poured the coffee, added the sugar, and headed into the kitchen for the pie. As Kristin sipped the coffee, she looked around. The town itself wasn't too dissimilar to Wealdstone, but everything seemed like it was frozen in time. The diner, the street layout, even the movie theatre across the way. Everything looked like it had been lifted from *Back to the Future*.

"Here you go honey."

The woman slid a large piece of pie across the counter to Kristin who nodded in thanks. She picked up the fork, but as she stabbed it into the pie crust, an image flashed in front of her eyes. She saw a brief impression of Daniella's mutilated body. One second, and it was gone. She shook her head, and placed the piece of pie into her mouth. As she brought the fork down into the pie again, another image. This time a flash of Kathryn transforming into some kind of black smoke creature, and a very distinct sensation of Kristin being ripped apart.

The fork clattered to the ground, and Kristin slammed her hand on the counter as she tried to steady herself. Several people were now looking at her, and the waitress sidled over to her.

"Are you alright, honey?" she asked, placing a hand on top of Kristin's.

But Kristin couldn't hear her. Her mind was racing with images and sensations of pain and suffering and anger. She saw herself being killed, murdered, torn apart, images of her loved ones dead before her. Everything that she had experienced in the Realm of Screams was now tearing through her mind like a bulldozer. Her fists clenched, and her fingernails punctured her palms. The waitress noticed trickles of blood coming from beneath the nails, and she tried to reach Kristin again.

"Oh my, please honey, you gotta stop!"

Then Kristin became still. The bombardment had reached maximum intensity. As the waitress again placed a hand on Kristin's, she grabbed the coffee pot from off the counter, and slammed it into the side of the waitress's head, glass shattering and tearing at her skin, and the hot coffee burning the areas the glass didn't cut. She screamed and dropped to the floor. Two truckers raced towards Kristin, but she delivered a gut punch to one, and an uppercut to the other. The second trucker collapsed through a table, and a broken shard of wood from the table leg pierced his thigh.

A third patron of the diner, approached Kristin from the side, and threw a punch across her jaw, sending her back into the counter, her head bouncing off the surface. And suddenly, she had clarity once more. She looked around at the destruction. She had no definitive memory of what had just happened. It was as if she had fallen asleep on the couch and woken up in hospital. The disorientation was overwhelming.

Behind her, she could hear people screaming for the police, and the agonising screams of the impaled man behind her. Her breathing was once again at a remarkably fast pace, and all she could think to do was leave. She rushed forwards, and flew out of the door to the diner. Narrowly avoiding oncoming traffic, she leapt into her car, started the engine, and screeched her way out of the parking space.

She didn't stop accelerating until she had burst past the town limits on the other side and found herself on the back roads. Once she was certain she was at least fifteen miles out of Wellsfield, she pulled the car to a sharp halt, and down off the side of the road. She gently turned the key and allowed the engine to die, and clambered out of the car. Kristin staggered forward into the woods a few hundred feet, and then fell against the side of a large tree catching her breath.

She tilted her head back and let out a guttural scream into the air, the sound reverberating all around her, her vocal chords straining with the effort. When she closed her mouth, she collapsed onto the floor, and began sobbing uncontrollably.

She now had confirmation.

The words that Ariella had spoken to her were now on a loop in her mind alongside all of the imagery.

"Mortals are not meant to enter our realm. Your bodies are not designed to cope with the experiences a Pain Wraith goes through."

So what exactly *had* happened to her while she was there. She experienced death over the course of a thousand lifetimes in a concentrated space of time. Something there had not only begun to unravel her mind, but alter her very makeup, her very existence. Whatever it was, she was now dangerous.

Then she remembered something. Ariella had been watching them before she got involved in the battle against Monarch. Surely, she would still be watching now.

"ARIELLA!" she screamed.

Nothing.

"ARIELLA! I know you're up there!"

Again nothing.

Nobody was coming to help her. She was on her own. But perhaps the others could help her make sense of it. Annie may have some knowledge of what to do, maybe she should head back to Wealdstone?

But no.

She could never go back.

She could never be around people again.

Kristin turned and slowly made her way back to the Mustang and climbed behind the wheel.

"Where can I go? What's happening to me?"

But of course, there was nobody to answer her.

And there wasn't going to be.

The Pain Wraiths were no longer watching.

She couldn't risk being around people.

She turned the key in the ignition, the engine breathed back into life, and she punched it. Tyres screeched sending dirt and gravel shooting into the air. As the rubber hit the road surface, tyre smoke billowed through the air, and the car vanished into the distance.

SEVEN

The basement, despite the usual nature of such places, was a vibrantly coloured area. In fact it appeared that it was one of the most recently renovated places in the entire facility. But this, however, was not a happy place. Kristin was tied to an upright table at a forty-five degree angle. A thick leather strap bound her to the table in four places.

One reached across her chest horizontally, one across her hips in the same direction, and one running over each shoulder meeting between her thighs and going back into a groove in the table. There was also a thinner strap running across her forehead, meaning she was completely incapacitated. Her wrists and ankles were also bound by zip ties to the metal loops at the side and base of the structure.

It would be clear to anyone outside of these walls, that this instrument was devised for one thing, and one thing only.

Torture.

The ocean green walls caught the thin strip lighting hanging from the ceiling and created a wave effect as they swayed. Two security guards stood either side of the only door into the room, and Christian was sat directly in front of Kristin. Alongside her, was an IV drip containing a bright orange liquid, and the solution was being fed directly into Kristin's arm.

For the last hour, Christian had used a combination of drugs and hypnotism to subdue Kristin, and forced her to tell him everything about the events leading up to her capture. So far, the details had been mildly interesting at best, but he suspected there was more she was hiding. He was still doubting what he himself had seen, but for the moment, it was the truth that he craved so badly. The desire to finally have his answers forcing him into taking this kind of action.

"Do you remember what happened after you drove away from Wellsfield?" he asked in as calm a voice as possible.

Kristin's eyes were in a permanent state of rolling around in her head. Sweat poured from her face. The room was a cold one but Kristin's skin was on fire. The guards had stripped her down to her underwear before strapping her to the table, very acutely aware of the effects these drugs would have on a subject. Christian had used this technique before and it had not ended well.

"I… I remember… a village. Small. Compact. I… I…"

Christian stood up from his chair, and walked around to her side, bringing his face closer to hers. He could feel the heat emanating from her.

"Yes Kristin, what do you remember?"

"I… got a sandwich. I was… I was hungry. Someone… a man… tried to rob them… blacked out… woke up and… everyone was dead."

It seemed that she had left quite a wake of destruction behind her. Wherever she went, something would trigger an animalistic behaviour and death would follow.

"How many places did you go to before you were arrested, Kristin?"

She flexed slightly against the restraints which were now more moveable with the moisture that had formed beneath them.

"Sixteen places… I bought a cabin… in the woods… away from people… tried to figure out…argh!"

With a swift and immediate change, Kristin snapped out of the hypnosis she had been under, and her breathing picked up. Christian glanced at the IV line, and the bag was empty. It was only effective whilst being administered, and he had clearly taken too long in his questioning. He returned to his seat.

"What the fuck are you doing to me?" she demanded, now fully in control of her thoughts.

Christian gestured to the empty bag to her left.

"I administered an experimental sedative into your system. It allows for immediate calm, and encourages the recipient to be honest. It's my own take on sodium pentothal. It was the only way I could be sure."

Kristin was becoming more agitated by the second, but she could not help but notice that the whirlwind of painful memories was nowhere in her mind. She needed to know more, and so decided to cooperate.

"Sure about what?"

"Sure that you weren't some black ops operative trying to shut me down."

Kristin scoffed.

"That would be a much easier situation."

Christian nodded.

"Yes. I can see from what you've told me that you do genuinely believe you experienced something truly harrowing. It has certainly toyed with your mind."

He stood once more, and grabbed a file from the nearby desk. Rather bizarrely, he then motioned for the two guards to leave the room.

"Are you sure Doctor? You've seen what she's capable of."

Despite their protests, he ushered them out and closed the door.

"I was able to get a report from a friend in the police department. He's been compiling a trail of where you've been and eyewitness accounts. He even tried to get in touch with your former wife, but wasn't successful. It would appear she is no longer in Wealdstone."

That last statement struck a chord with Kristin.

"What do you mean she's not in Wealdstone anymore?"

Christian was taken aback by the response. From everything Kristin had told him during her induced hypnosis, she felt nothing but resentment towards her wife.

"Simply put, your wife and her partner, moved away. No trace. Nobody knows where they are."

Kristin's mind was racing now that it was free of her previously unmoveable torture. Why would they have left without leaving any indication of reason or destination? That however would have to wait.

"This drug you've given me... what exactly did you put in it?"

Now Christian's curiosity was peaked.

"Why do you ask?"

Kristin took a deep breath, before trying to explain.

"My mind is unravelling. Ever since what happened to me in Wealdstone, and... elsewhere, I've been bombarded by build ups of painful memories, feelings of extreme agony, and frequent bouts of rage. The horrors in my mind were on a merry-go-round, always there, just waiting to spin fast enough that they took over, and resulted in the kinds of violence you've seen of me. But right now, I feel nothing. No pain. No agony. No violent thoughts. So I'll ask you again, Doctor. What did you put in there?"

Christian was now open mouthed. Had he accidentally stumbled on some kind of alleviation for the strongest of his patient's mental afflictions? He immediately ran over to the bag, and unhooked it from the stand it was hanging on, and removed the line from Kristin's arm.

"I knew it was experimental, and it hasn't been certified, but I had no idea there would be side effects like this!"

Kristin did not care for his newfound excitement, and it was only as his coat brushed against her thigh that she realised she was less than fully clothed.

"Where are my clothes, you pervert?" she shouted.

Christian waved away her protests as he carried the bag over to the desk to examine it more closely. He attempted to try and recount the steps that had gone into creating the serum, but as he did so, the room seemed to darken slightly. Kristin noticed it too.

"Doctor, you need to let me out of here right now!"

He turned around and saw one of the lights begin to flicker.

"Not again."

Kristin's head, which had now managed to slide free of the head restraint, snapped in his direction.

"What?" she asked, her voice ending in a higher pitch.

Christian ignored her, and began to back away from the light that was now malfunctioning. Kristin addressed him again.

"You've seen it, haven't you?" she asked.

Christian got angry.

"I haven't seen anything! I can't have seen it! Why is it here?"

That hadn't quite been the response that Kristin had expected. That inferred that Christian was familiar with this entity somehow.

"Doc, I need you to tell me where you saw this thing."

Christian rubbed his eyes with his palms, but it didn't alter anything. The black twisting mass was beginning to form in the corner of the room, above the door next to the light.

"This morning, when you went more batshit crazy than normal! It was above you the whole time!"

There was something more there.

"Doc, when else have you seen this?"

Christian, rather unexpectedly, began to shed tears, his face contorting into a depiction of pure terror as the mass began to grow.

"DOC?"

"It… it was in my house… three weeks ago! I thought I'd… I'd imagined it, but then I saw it here this morning, and now it's… it's coming for me isn't it?"

Kristin actually managed a small sarcastic chuckle.

"Actually, I thought it was coming for me."

The mass grew further, but unlike previous sightings, began to twist and move downwards as if it was trying to form an actual presence.

"Doc, you really need to let me out of here!"

Then all of the lights blew out.

There was the smallest hint of light still coming through the door from the corridor lights outside, but the only sound was of Christian's heavy and panicked breathing, and Kristin's heartbeat. She was trying to hold her breath, and squinted her eyes. She saw what appeared to be slight shimmer as something moved ahead of her. A low, dull whine began to emanate from the entity, which now moved to block the light of the door.

"Wh… what do you want from me?"

Christian's voice had now become the opposite to the dominance he had shown when he believed he was in complete control.

"Shut up, Doc," came Kristin's reply.

A loud shriek then filled the room, as the twisting, oily mass parted to create what looked like a large mouth, and shot towards Christian.

As the noise became so loud, the table Kristin was lying on vibrated, the door was kicked in and the two security guards burst back into the room. The entity halted its pursuit and turned towards them. Immediately, they opened fire, but the bullets flew straight through it, two of them impacting on Christian's chest, knocking him to the floor.

The creature lunged at the guards, and appeared to separate itself into two, making it able to strike both guards simultaneously. They were thrown into opposing walls, and the creature shot back up onto the ceiling and retreated into the corner until it was gone.

Kristin struggled against the restraints furiously, but could only loosen them. But then something she feared began to happen. The painful binding she had carried inside her mind for a year, began to slowly trickle back in. Whatever numbing effect the experimental drugs had had on her, were now wearing off.

"No, no, NO!"

She screamed so loudly, that footsteps could be heard in the corridor. As all of the painful feelings came rushing back, two more guards, and a nurse entered the room.

That was the last thing Kristin remembered before she blacked out on the table.

EIGHT

The lights in Christian's office were at their maximum levels. Thank goodness for dimmable lights, he thought to himself. He had absolutely no desire to be in any form of darkness right now. He had definitely had his fill of that for the day.

He glanced towards the clock on his wall, and sighed as it ticked over to nine p.m. Normally, he would be home by now, enjoying a glass of Haig, and watching the latest episode of *Yellowstone*, identifying with the dominant characters on the screen and trying to adapt them to his own personality. In that respect, he was very much a false individual. He was also an incredibly damaged individual, and he often thought that if he were not in charge of the Moriarty Hospital, he would have become a patient himself.

The ringing of the telephone made Christian leap out of his chair, and drop the now luke warm cup of coffee he had managed to pour himself. As the dark liquid seeped into the cream coloured rug beneath his feet, he cautiously moved back towards the phone, and picked up the receiver.

"H-hello?" he asked tentatively.

"Hello Dr Verne, this is Detective Frank Short."

Christian felt a cold chill shoot up his spine. He prided himself on keeping activities in the hospital quiet, but a call from the cops was the last thing he needed right now.

"H-how… how can I help you Detective?"

There was a brief pause on the other end of the line.

"Are you okay, Doctor? You sound… troubled."

Christian launched himself back down into his chair in an effort to be more comfortable and attempted to put on his brave voice, that he usually saved for the boardroom level assholes.

"Yes, everything is fine, Detective. What leads you to call so late?"

A snort came from the other end of the line.

"Well, I've received a rather unusual request on my desk tonight. About a year ago, me and my partner Detective Ford, attended the scene of a multiple homicide and arson involving a rather well known person."

A quiver returned to Christian's voice. He knew exactly of the incident Detective Short was referring to.

"Yes, I think I remember that. Made the local news as I recall."

Another pause. Christian sensed that the detective was trying to gauge his responses, and in his current state of mind, Christian was not entirely certain he was covering his tracks particularly well.

"Yes, well the person in question was a Mrs. Kristin Silverton, or should I say Ms. Kristin Booth as she is no longer married. Me and my partner visited her in the hospital at the time, and she was obviously in extreme distress, and I believe she was committed to your facility just three weeks later, is that correct?"

Christian cleared his throat.

"Yes, that is correct. I remember admitting her myself."

"Uh-huh. That's good, Doc. Because the request that has come across my desk tonight, is to have her released."

Christian nearly dropped the telephone. His left leg involuntarily collapsed despite him putting very little weight on it as he leaned over his desk. He quickly regained his composure, but his face told a different story. He was extremely glad that Detective Short could not see him.

"I'm sorry, could you repeat that?"

"We've had a request from a high priority contact that demands her immediate release. It's come with all the necessary signatures and stamps, so it's my duty to just pass that to you. Is Ms. Booth still in your facility?"

Christian fell silent. He needed to know more about everything going on at Moriarty, and he knew Kristin was linked to it somehow. He had absolutely no intention of letting her go. He didn't care who was demanding for her release.

"No. She is not currently housed here."

Christian could hear paper shuffling in the background, before Detective Short spoke again.

"When was she transferred? I don't have any record of her moving to another facility."

This time, Christian was quicker.

"No, you misunderstand me, Detective. Ms. Silver- Ms. Booth, has not been transferred, she has simply been taken to another hospital for additional treatment. She should be back with us inside of a week."

Christian knew that there was no way he had a week to find out everything he needed to know, or that the detective on the other end of the phone line believed a word he said. He was however confident his lie would buy him some time.

"What is the name of the facility, Doctor?"

Shit.

That caught Christian out. He needed to continue thinking on his feet, or it was over.

"I'm afraid I cannot disclose that to you, Detective. It is a confidential facility for high risk patients. Anonymity is a requirement."

He had no idea where he had dug that from, but the response surprisingly had the desired effect.

"Very well, Doc. I'll be sending the papers overnight, so you should get them by close of day tomorrow. And Doc, I wanna be notified the second Ms. Booth walks back through your doors. Understood?"

How dare this desk pushing fool dictate how Christian conducts his business. This was *his* facility. Nothing that happened within these walls was the business of anybody else. This was his domain and he was king here.

"Listen to me very carefully, Detective. The care and treatment of my patients is of my concern, and not yours. I operate under a complete confidentiality arrangement. If I find these papers legitimate, I will respond to your request. But until then, I am in charge of what happens here. Do I make myself clear?"

Silence on the other end.

"Detective?"

The sound of a cigarette drag flowed down the line.

"Yeah I get you, Doc. Loud and clear."

The line went dead.

Christian was no longer certain his outburst had delivered the desired effect. But right now, he didn't have much choice. Something was in his hospital. People were dying. Kristin was somehow linked to whatever this creature was. But the fact that the initial sighting in his home had turned out to not be a drunken hallucination, was the aspect terrifying him the most.

Why was it here, and what did it want? And more to the point, why could nobody but Kristin seem to see it? Even the guards it slammed out of the way had not seen what attacked them. And as for Kristin, her behaviour and strength was now growing to the point where he was unsure how much longer they could contain her.

The release request had taken him by surprise. Who had submitted the request and why? One thing was for certain, he did not have time to deliberate. It was time to take this interrogation to the next level. One way or another, Kristin would give him the answers he needed. And he knew just the person for the job.

NINE

Kristin was unsure of where she had been taken, but it certainly wasn't her room at the end of the corridor back on the Wealdstone wing. It was brighter, and even had a large window on the back wall, looking out over the courtyard. The only details she remembered about the harrowing night before, was the calming effect Christian's drugs had given her for a brief period of time, and then the darkness. The swirling demonic presence returning to her, but this time she had not been alone.

It was as if it was targeting Christian.

The aggression that it had displayed was new to her. As was the fact that somebody else had seen it. And there was another detail she had retained before the rage had caused her latest blackout. This malevolent force had visited his home.

She had many questions for the good doctor when she next saw him. But she feared that would not be too far away, and that given his previous methods, it would not be a pleasant one. Part of her felt it may be more beneficial to enter one of her crazed states, and try to break out of here, but the pain was too much and however bad things were, she had no desire to willingly conjure it.

What she did decide to do, was scout the room to try and figure out where she was. The door seemed to be made of lighter steel, and had a traditional wooden frame around it. That wasn't a very smart idea, considering she had been told by one of the nurses that she managed to smash a four inch steel door off of its hinges in the last attack. Scanning around, her bare feet smacking on the unfamiliar red tiles on the floor, she noticed the ceiling tiles were made of polystyrene, and was only around a foot higher than her head. Again, that seemed too relaxed compared to the usual intense security measures she had experienced thus far. But surely the window would be bullet proof right?

Wrong.

She noticed a small handle concealed in the window frame. Lifting it, the window swung open. All the way open.

"This must be a trick," she said aloud. "This isn't funny guys."

It was only at this point, that she realised that her voice was not her own. There was no breeze flowing in from the open window, and there were no sounds either.

"What the…"

Kristin looked down, but these feet were not hers. The hands she now turned over and back, were not her own. She ran those hands over her body, but that was neither hers, or recognisable. Feeling her chest, she managed to conjure a flippant remark.

"Well these definitely aren't mine."

Suddenly, a stab of pain shot through her temple, and she dropped to one knee. It was when she opened her eyes that she saw an alien face looking back at her. The shiny red surface of the floor tiles confirmed what she had suspected. Staring back at her was a woman, mid-twenties at most, ebony skin, and hair which reached beyond her shoulders. Kristin moved her left arm and ran her hand over her lips. The reflection mimicked the movements.

"This is some serious *Quantum Leap* type shit."

The voice of the woman was similar in pitch to her own, but different enough to make her feel uncomfortable. Another shot to the side of the head sent her crashing to the floor onto her side. But this time, when she opened her eyes, she was no longer in the body of the woman.

Kristin was now standing in the corner of the room looking at the body she had just inhabited. And the scene had changed dramatically. The window was now closed, rain lashing the glass from the outside, the room was darker, one of the lights above the woman no longer illuminated.

Kristin watched as the woman was struck in the face by an assailant who had just appeared in the room. Kristin could not explain the man's entrance to the scene. One second he was not there, she blinked, and suddenly he was there. He struck the woman in the side of the head for a fourth time. Almost in response, Kristin felt the sharp pain in her own temple, as she had done when she inhabited the body in front of her.

"Please! Stop!"

The cries of the woman were spoken through increased and borderline hysterical breathing. The man, who still had his back to her, said nothing. He grabbed her by the arm, and dragged her up to meet his face, before delivering direct and powerful headbutt to her nose, which exploded with blood as she was sent careering backwards, smacking the back of her head on the wall.

The sound was sickening, and a thin trail of blood streaked down the wall as she slid to the ground, still conscious, but barely. Each impact registered with Kristin, and she too found herself slumped on the floor, but unable to take her eyes away from the events before her.

The man lumbered forward, and knelt down in front of her. Reaching forwards, he grabbed her by the throat, and pinned her head upright against the wall.

"Tell me everything you know, and I'll make this easy for you."

The man's gruff voice was incredibly low. So much so, that the vibrations of his words rumbled along the hard tiled floor. Kristin felt the tightness around her throat, mimicking everything the young woman was going through. She tried to form words, but just couldn't get them out. He loosened his grip slightly, and asked again.

"Dr Verne didn't want to go this far, Naomi. But you forced him. You made this happen. It's your fault. Now tell me what I want to know, or this is going to get much more unpleasant for you."

The woman who Kristin now knew was called Naomi, burst into hysterics. She couldn't have formed any words if she had chosen to. The feeling of intense pain, fear, confusion, and loss was resonating through both her mind, and Kristin's. But the man's patience had long since departed. He let go of Naomi, who instinctively coiled up into a ball, and he walked over to the window, pulling a cell phone from his pocket. Kristin saw that the phone was of an older design, and still had a small aerial protruding from the top. This now became a case of not where she was, but *when* she was. Judging from the fact the man, who had still not yet shown his face, had not seen her, she believed she was reliving a memory. This was nothing new to her after her thousand lifetimes of death and misery she experience in the Realm of Screams, but this felt different. She was not reliving her own memories, but those of someone else.

But who was the someone else?

Clearly, the memory was not Naomi's because she could see her crouched on the floor.

Neither was it that of the beastly man before her, for the same reason.

"Dr Christian Verne please."

The man was now on the phone, and was clearly speaking to a receptionist or personal assistant. There was a brief pause.

"Doctor, I'm afraid Naomi is not forthcoming with her knowledge."

A long pause, during which the man nodded twice.

"I understand. I will be ten minutes. Then you may send the crew in. I will be gone by then."

The man pressed a button on the phone and it beeped with acknowledgement that the phone call had ended. For the first time, the man turned enough so Kristin could see his face. He was in fact bald, with light stubble atop his head. On his chin was a thick grey and white peppered beard, and his eyes glimmered with each flash of lightning that struck outside beyond the walls of the facility. She estimated he was around forty-five, and his face was weathered. If she didn't know better, she would've guessed he was formerly in one of the armed services. He had the look of a man who had seen warfare. And death.

What happened next left Kristin rooted to the spot in shock.

The man reached down, and hauled Naomi to her feet, and pressed her against the wall. He pinned her there until she stood of her own volition. He then grabbed very small sections of her clothing, and tore it open. He was attempting to make it appear she had snagged her clothing on something, branches perhaps.

He then lifted her clean off the floor, turned her sideways, and launched her through the glass window, which shattered into several large jagged pieces, the sound of Naomi's limp body landing on the concrete audible despite the heavy rain.

The man then climbed through the window, and jumped down onto the hard surface outside. Kristin could not move. She could just about see the arms of the man rising and falling, making sharp movements, but everything was happening below the window level.

Moments later, as she began to feel the spray of the rain now entering through the broken window, she saw the man lift Naomi's clearly dead body onto his shoulders. She was sporting dozens of lacerations to both her exposed flesh, and through additional cuts through her tattered clothes. Clearly this beast was attempting to depict a fictional scene of some sort. Kristin watched him march away into the rain until she could see him no more.

Her legs twitched, and she was finally able to take a step forward, but she only took the one. Behind her, she felt a cold breath on her neck and she froze once more. Carefully, she turned around and what she saw absolutely terrified her to her very core. Standing on the other side of the door looking through the window was Doctor Christian. His eyes were vacant, younger, but tortured.

He looked straight through her, obviously unaware of her presence, and she saw he held a similar cell phone in her hand to the one the killer had used. It was at this point that she wondered if this was *his* memory that she was reliving. But how was that possible?

Then it became clear.

Standing just behind Christian, also with a clear view through the large window in the door, was a woman. She held her hand over her mouth, and tears were streaming down her face. From the overwhelming sadness now taking effect within Kristin, she realised that the memory belonged to this woman. The fact she was looking back at her rather than within her no longer had any relevance. She could feel it. She knew.

The woman took a sharp breath in, and Christian was alerted to her presence, and span around.

"No. No, no, no, no, please no. Angie, I can explain!"

The woman turned and ran towards a nearby staircase, and turned to clamber up the steps. Kristin now found herself standing alongside the railings, seemingly pulled along by the memory on display.

"Get the fuck away from me Christian! You're a monster!"

Christian grabbed at the woman, who wrestled away from him, but he increased his speed and followed her half way up the staircase before grabbing hold of her again, and slamming her against the staircase wall.

"Angie, please! I had to know what she knew! What she had seen! I was… I was protecting us!"

Angie tried to pull away from him, but his grip was stronger than she had expected.

"You're crazy! The way you treat these people, the way you hurt them! You should be locked up in one of these cells, NOT these people!"

Christian lost his cool, and backhanded Angie across the face. She let out a small scream which seemed to encourage Christian, whose eyes were now bulging, the whites dominant in his gaze.

"You are meant to support me. You're my wife Angie. What we do, we do together. What we start, we finish together!"

Angie pulled something out of her purse and lunged at Christian, the slight sound of tearing fabric audible to Kristin, still stood at the foot of the stairs. Angie withdrew her hand which was now covered in blood, and Kristin could see the shine of a small blade. Christian looked down at his wound, before returning his fading gaze to his wife.

Without another word being said, he fell backwards, and tumbled down the stairs, and as he hit each one, Kristin heard a bone crack. Ribs, arm, and finally hand as he landed at the bottom with a thud, and a gash on his head. His phone clattered beside him, and his eyes closed.

Angie ran up the rest of the stairs and vanished from view, and the scene began to fade. Just as the view faded to black, Kristin saw Christian's hand reach for the phone.

TEN

In the initial stage of being awakened by the harsh reality of the cold water splashing against her face, Kristin managed to squint enough to see the black entity retreat across the ceiling into the far corner of the room. The second bucket of water though, took her breath away.

"Wake up."

The voice in question had the opposite effect. Kristin stayed exactly where she was, almost afraid to look up.

"I said…"

A sharp and intense pain shot through her ribs as the boot made contact and she was sent rolling onto her back.

"…wake up!"

Kristin burst into an uncontrollable cough as she attempted to get the air back into her lungs.

"Good. Now let's begin."

The gruff man from her vision grabbed her by both arms and lifted her clear off the ground, strolled across the room, and slammed her down onto a chair. The impact reverberated throughout her entire body, and a dull ache settled in her head, quietly pulsing away amongst the crowded room of her mind.

The man backed away and stopped approximately five feet away, folding his hands across his chest. He was much bigger in person, and as strong as Kristin had once been, in her now fragile state, she was intimidated by him. Experiencing what he had done to somebody else did not exactly enhance her feelings towards this man either, but right now she needed to focus. The images were stirring again.

"My name is Kenrick. I'm here to extract information from you. Dr Christian is on somewhat of a shortened timeframe, and we don't have time to pussyfoot around."

Kenrick.

Well at least she now knew the monster's name. She did notice that his face appeared not too dissimilar from his visage in his previous appearance. Slightly more white in the beard than before and more wrinkles around the eyes, but that was more or less it.

"What exactly do you need from me?" she asked.

Kenrick took a deep breath.

"I've been given an… unusual set of questions to ask you. Normally when I am called in to assist the good doctor, it's fairly straightforward. What did you see? What did you hear? Who else knows about this? Fairly simple stuff. But this… this is different."

Kristin let slip a small chuckle, which she immediately regretted. Luckily, Kenrick did not take action.

"He wants to know about the entity, doesn't he?" she asked.

Kenrick's eyebrows raised and for a slight moment, his guard broke. Kristin suspected he didn't think it would be this easy to convey the unusual situation he now found himself in.

"As a matter of fact, he does. He would like to know what *you* know about it. From what he can tell, only the two of you can see this… twisting black mass."

Kristin let out another little chuckle, but she didn't get away with it twice. Kenrick raised his right leg, and without too much effort, slammed it into Kristin's chest, sending both her and the chair careering backwards. She gasped desperately for air, whilst trying to soothe her mind at the same time.

As she regained some form of focus, she felt herself slammed back down in the now righted chair. Kenrick leaned in to her face.

"Please understand, Ms. Silverton, I am in charge here. I have heard about your bouts of violence and seemingly infinite strength, and I can tell you that there is no way you come out of this a winner."

He backed away again to the same exact spot he had been on before, and once again crossed his arms.

"Oh yeah, you're definitely ex-military. Too precise. Too efficient, and despite the brutality, very polite."

To her surprise, Kenrick smiled. That admittedly caught her off guard. He seemed to relax a little.

"You're a very observant woman, Ms. Silverton. You are of course correct. I served fifteen years in the United States Marines, before being drafted into a more, shall we say, independent operation. I have seen so much death and destruction, I have become somewhat desensitised to it. Not much makes me squirm."

Kristin had seen evidence of that first hand. She was desperately trying to suppress the rising rage within her and keep her focus, but every day it became harder and harder, and the treatment she was being shown seemed to be accelerating the process. Surprisingly, Kenrick seemed to notice this.

"Oh yes, the superhuman rage. Doctor Christian provided me with something to help that particular affliction."

He stomped his way towards her, and with his right hand grabbed her by the hair, twisting her head to the side, and with his left, reached into his jacket pocket, extracted a long syringe, and plunged the contents into Kristin's neck.

He removed the needle, tossed it into a nearby trash can, and returned to his spot. Kristin felt a fire rushing through her veins, as if a heavy barrage of raging water was tearing it's way down the side of a burst dam. Her head shook from side to side rapidly as the mystery serum took effect, and then as quickly as she had been injected, she fell silent.

Her head was once more at ease. No images of pain, no images of death and no instant recall of those memories from her torturous experience.

"You're gonna have to tell me what he puts in that," she joked between laboured breaths.

She did however, feel her temperature rising exponentially, and in mere seconds, the sweat was visible on her face and through her white hospital issued vest top.

"I don't believe it's a family recipe, but nevertheless I think it's probably going to remain a need to know formula."

Kristin tilted her head to the side and nodded gently.

"Worth a shot."

Kenrick tensed himself up and returned her to the matter at hand.

"Now, tell me everything you know about this entity."

Kristin looked at him, and in the corner of the room, she could see it. Restricted almost entirely to the darkest corner, but just visible enough to let her know it was there. She wondered if it was eyeing up Kenrick, or whether it was afraid of him. It was also at this point that she noticed, the entity was not entirely black in colour. This was the brightest a room had been when the creature was present, and she saw it had much more of a turquoise hue to its construction.

"Ms. Silverton?"

Kenrick reminded her that he did not have the patience for delays.

"I didn't see it until I was brought here. I was having my own issues without anything else coming up."

Kenrick was listening intently.

"The superhuman violence issues," he surmised.

Kristin nodded.

"Yeah that's the stuff. Being tortured for a thousand lifetimes kinda has that effect on a girl, you know? Anyways, the first time I saw it was in the showers last week. Now I've been here a year, and I hadn't seen it until then. Crept up on me after one of my… blackouts."

The creature in the corner of the room seemed to be reacting to Kristin recounting the story, and she locked eyes on it. Again, Kenrick didn't fail to notice this subtle change, but did not break his gaze.

"Please, continue."

Kristin tried to look away from the swirling mass, but she couldn't. It was almost as if it was trying to tap into her mind, but was finding nothing. She felt a probing presence searching for something. It felt as if someone was looking behind a series of closed doors but finding the rooms empty. It seemed to react negatively the longer it went on.

"Yeah, so I basically freaked out and when I woke up, I'd killed one of the guards. I saw it retreating across the ceiling as they dragged me away."

"And after that?"

Kristin watched as the entity slowly crept further out of the shadows, before stopping once more.

"The next time was the following night. I thought I was dreaming. It let me out of my cell, and I stood in the corridor, watching it crawl along the ceiling towards me. It stopped by Nat's room. Then I woke up."

Kenrick scratched his beard.

"Nat? The young woman who was found dead the next morning?"

Kristin nodded.

"I had only spoken to her a couple of times. She told me how she'd been possessed by a demon in Trinity Bay, and how she always felt like someone was watching her. I guess she was right."

The mass in the corner of the room lashed out into the air. One tendril took a swipe towards Kristin, but failed to reach her. Nevertheless she jumped a little in her chair. Kenrick did glance this time towards the corner of the room, but confused at seeing nothing, looked back at Kristin.

"And then?"

Kristin forced herself to look away from the entity, and fixed her gaze on the floor.

"I don't remember. I just woke up in the middle of the corridor, surrounded by dead guards, blood… and Doctor Verne. He was staring at the ceiling, his eyes were just… gone. Like whatever he saw had grabbed him by the throat and wouldn't let go. Then they knocked me out."

Kenrick walked across to a nearby countertop, and poured a glass of water from a jug. He downed the entire glass, and then once again returned to his spot. Kristin noticed a few scattered beads of sweat forming on top of his bald head. She herself was now drenched in perspiration, but Kenrick pressed for more.

"I was told that the doctor saw the same entity you described, hovering above you in the hallway when you were at your most destructive. But I want to know when *you* next saw it."

Kristin's mind was beginning to wander. The constant probing she felt within her head was now beginning to smash down the barricades that Doctor Vern's serum had erected.

"I… I don't… I can't remember…"

Kenrick began to tense up. Up until now, he had felt relatively calm. Certainly calm enough not to restrain Kristin despite her reputation. But something wasn't quite right.

"Ms. Silverton, I will not tolerate any games. Tell me what else you know."

He took two steps towards her before stopping. Kristin was struggling to keep her focus.

"I… I saw it in the basement. When I was being held… the first time this serum was administered to me… it… it didn't want me that time… it wanted… him."

Kenrick watched as her eyes flicked back and forth as if watching a sped-up tennis match. The tension in her now balled up fists was turning her knuckles white. She continued muttering.

"It… he said it followed him home… was worried it wanted something from him… it attacked him… but it called to me… I…"

Kristin threw her head to the side, and then to the other side. The veins in her neck began to pop and they streaked down her neck beneath her shirt, and all the way up to her temple in the other direction. Kenrick was becoming unsettled. If he didn't have such drilled training, he would believe something was attempting to invade Kristin.

"What's happening? Do not try and play games with me, Ms. Silverton."

Kristin ignored her interrogator, and continued to thrash around, her arms now flailing. Kenrick had tolerated enough. He advanced on her and grabbed her by the throat, lifting her off the chair, but she continued to thrash around. A low guttural growl began to emanate from her throat. Kenrick raised his free hand and swung it towards Kristin's jaw.

Her hand shot up to stop it.

As Kenrick watched, Kristin's focus seemed absolute. Her head lifted up, and her eyes were consumed by violet lights, flashing in her retinas like bolts of lightning. The actual whites of her eyes had turned black. She held Kenrick's fist in the air with little to no effort. He tried to pull it away, but it was locked in her grasp.

"Ms. Silverton! Stop this!"

Kristin's teeth clenched together, she looked him dead in the eye, and placed her other hand against his throat.

"My name… is Kristin Booth!"

She bellowed the sentence into Kenrick's face, spittle flying against his skin, and she squeezed his neck so hard, all of the bones within it crunched together, and his face turned ghostly white. The veins along his neck and face became visible, and as he glanced upwards, he could see the turquoise mass swirling directly above Kristin.

Kristin removed her hand from his throat as the last of his life left his body, and they both collapsed to the floor, Kenrick's body lying in a heap, eyes wide open and bloodshot, and Kristin landing on her feet, slightly crouched as if she had jumped from a height.

As her feet touched the ground, the violet light vanished from her eyes, and she was once more herself. She looked around the room, but saw no sign of the demonic creature that had been inhabiting the ceiling for the duration of their time together.

She glanced down at Kenrick's lifeless body, and for the first time, felt no sadness. No remorse. He had been a monster, and he deserved to die. However, this time, she also remembered every detail. This had not been a blackout. This had been an almost liberating experience. She caught her reflection in a nearby glass cabinet, and she felt a smile etch its way onto her face.

She had once again taken a life.

But this time, it had brought her pleasure.

ELEVEN

The surge now running through Kristin's body made her feel like she was charging with electricity. The imagery spinning around in her mind was now pushed to the back almost as if those images themselves were a power station. Her skin tingled, and the dopamine was incredible. Instinctively, she reached her hand forwards, and gave the air a sharp tug, and in response, the door to the room was ripped from its hinges and flew behind her.

The smile on her face grew wider, and she slowly strolled her way into the corridor. It seemed like something within her had activated. She no longer cared what it was, or where it had come from. She just wanted more. *Needed* more.

Two guards moved towards her, and she raised both arms, thrusting them forward and the two men dropped their weapons, grasping at their throats as if held by an invisible force. Kristin clenched her fists in the same way she had done with Kenrick, and their fate was the same. Their necks were compressed and crushed, and they dropped to the floor, a small trickle of blood flowing from their mouths.

"I wonder…" she said softly.

She paused, and stretched out both her arms, placing the palms of her hands on the shiny walls either side of the narrow corridor, and closed her eyes. The walls began to vibrate in response to her touch, before pulses of purple energy surged along them and off into the distance. The channels of light broke apart at the entrance to every room, and burst through the door in question, striking the occupant within directly in the centre of the chest. Within seconds, they exhibited the same smile currently on Kristin's face.

As the violet beam of possession flew around the facility, every patient began pounding at their cell door, in rhythm, one thud after another. However, back in the depths of the facility, Kristin's smile began to fade, as did her grip on the walls. The beams of violet energy began to dissipate, and just moments later, she collapsed forward onto the floor, gasping for breath.

All of the patients who had briefly been controlled by her newfound power, fell to the floor in their cells, confused by what had just happened. Kristin's power was depleted.

For now.

It took about fifteen minutes before Dr Christian and his team flew down to her location. Although dismayed at the sight before him, Christian was not surprised. He knew employing his old friend was a risk. He had not come up against the likes of her before, but he had been confident his sedative serum would subdue her as it had done previously. Clearly he was wrong.

Kristin's actions did surprise him, however. She voluntarily lay on the floor with her hands behind her back, and allowed herself to be restrained. When she was lifted to her feet, she asked to speak to him, and he nodded in agreement.

"Take her to my office. Four men on the door outside, and two inside until she is restrained."

The guards nodded, and carried her away. Christian surveyed the scene. More bodies to try and explain away. Kenrick had not been just another guard. He was a tool. And now he too was dead. As he looked upon the body of his old friend, he could not help flash back to the previous times he had required Kenrick's services, and felt a pang of guilt. That however, was soon overcome by the usual justification offered by his brain, that it was all to keep his career and reputation safe.

Time was running out, and he still did not have the answers he required. This was his final chance to get to the bottom of all of this before it was too late.

TWELVE

"Dinner time."

The three bangs on the door were a welcome sound for patient 141. He had been hungry for most of the day. Around two p.m. he had begun to sense his stomach eating itself, and felt the build up of the bile within. But as usual, all of the staff were freaking out about whatever was happening with patient 47, and were far too busy to look after everyone else.

141 had become accustomed to neglect, and had gotten used to the fact that he was simply a number to the staff within these walls, and so used everyone's numbers to identify them. There were no names in his mind anymore. Only numbers.

The door swung open, and guard 14871 slid the tray into the room, and swiftly closed the door again, knocking over the carton of milk which had been situated on the edge of the tray. 141 rushed forward to return it to an upright position, and dragged the tray and its contents across to his bed. 141 had been incarcerated here for almost eight years now. He was not insane. He was simply misunderstood.

His hands moved as if they were a blur, reorganising the food on his plate, and the plastic cutlery as his eyes flicked back and forth as if analysing the image before him. When he was done, he lowered his hands and observed what he had created.

The mashed potatoes, beef and other vegetables had been arranged into some kind of twisted ribbon construction. He looked at it, and smiled. Then he raised his head to the ceiling and stared at the entity floating above him on the ceiling.

"I hope you like it," he said, smiling.

The creature launched down from the ceiling and completely encompassed him. The screams of patient 141 could be heard down the corridor, but with everything going on elsewhere, nobody came, and nobody listened to the cries of those who still had most of their mental faculties that something was wrong.

One of the patients across the hall, now had their face pressed against the small window in their door. As they watched, patient 141's face was slammed against his window. His eyes were hollow and black, his skin clung tightly to his bones, and blood smeared the glass as he slid down out of sight. The man opposite now shook in terror as he saw the ribbons of teal and black twisting in such a way, it appeared to be expanding.

It had feasted. Dinner time indeed.

But as it began to manifest into a familiar shape, the man across the hall began to back away from his window. The tendrils of black and turquoise twisted and folded into each other, until a humanoid shape began to form. What resembled a head suddenly snapped in his direction. There were pits in the construction where eyes would normally be. As the man began to scream, the entity launched upwards out of sight.

A few moments began to pass, and nothing happened. The man moved back towards his window and gazed through the glass. Looking left and right, there was no evidence of any wrongdoing except for the small trickle of blood on the window of patient 141's cell door.

There was no audible sound as the creature lowered itself down through the ceiling behind him. A series of strands assembled themselves into a vertical 3D shape. Before he could sense its presence, his legs were pulled from under him and he vanished from view.

His screams joined the echoes around the corridor, as one by one the patients in the Wealdstone wing were consumed.

THIRTEEN

The atmosphere was different this time. The last few times Kristin had been in this office, she had very much felt confined, and in danger of those immediately around her. This time, however, she felt like she was the one in control. Something was awakening within her, and whilst previously, she had felt all of the painful reminders and pictures in her mind were slowly killing her, now she felt like she was in control of them and not the other way around.

Christian on the other hand, looked the most vulnerable she had ever seen him. He was stood next to his window, tie loosened, pale, sweating, looking through the glass as if he was expecting company.

"I don't know what to say to you, Kristin."

She wasn't expecting that statement to come from a man who personally oversaw her torture for almost a year.

"How about I ask you something instead, Doc?"

He looked towards her with almost relief on his face. He needed to know anything and everything about this entity, why it was coming for him and why it was so attracted to her, and yet he felt the burden of extracting those answers was no longer on his shoulders.

"Go on."

Kristin straightened herself in her chair and looked him directly in the eyes.

"What do *you* know about this thing? I want you to be honest with me, and I'll be honest with you. I think we're past the doctor patient torture bullshit."

Christian scoffed, but nodded. It was true. Their relationship now needed to change. Time was of the essence, and he could no longer conceal all of the death in his facility. The truth surrounding the circumstances of these murders would soon come to light. The time had come. There was no saving himself now.

"Very well."

He walked across to his chair, and briefly stared down at the coffee stain on his rug which was now dried. Just like his career, he thought to himself. Stained beyond repair. It had all been for nothing. He lowered himself into the chair, and nodded at the two guards inside to leave. They did so this time without hesitation. They had all seen what Kristin could do and were no longer as inclined to protect the doctor as they once had been.

"I saw it in my home. It was about a month before you were admitted here. I got home from the hospital one night, after a rather… difficult day, and I sat on my couch, and flicked on the TV. There was a news report about some plane crash near Wealdstone, and I remember thinking to myself how there may as well be a news channel dedicated to that shithole at this point."

Kristin rolled her eyes, but kind of understood what he meant. They had certainly made headlines over the last decade one way or another. And that was just the public view of the action. They still had no idea of the full details.

"We like to remind people we still exist."

Christian laughed.

"Yeah, well you're doing a bang up job of that."

Kristin returned the laugh, but never broke her gaze, reminding him that things had changed, and she was in charge despite her restraints. He got the message and continued.

"As I said, it had been a particularly hard day, and so I hit the nearest bottle. By the time the news bulletin was over, so were the contents of that bottle."

Kristin couldn't remember the last time she was in a relaxed enough state to watch TV let alone sit and enjoy a glass of something indulgent. No. She could remember. Her last drink had been in Will's bar in Trinity Bay before everything went awry. But the last time she felt relaxed and enjoyed a drink was at Sisko's in the aftermath of Jasmine's attack four years ago, surrounded by her friends. It seemed an eternity away at this point. Almost another lifetime. Christian was now looking into the distance at nothing specific. Kristin knew he was living in that memory, and didn't interrupt.

"Then I saw it. It just sort of seeped through the ceiling. At first I thought it was a leak from the bathroom upstairs, but the larger it grew, the more I realised it was something else. It writhed around like waves in the ocean. I swear it had a blue-green tint to it, but in the moment it looked more black. Then the phone rang, and it kind of shrank away quickly. I don't remember answering the phone, and the next thing I knew, I was waking up, still on the couch, empty bottle beside me. I just thought it was a dream, or a result of the whiskey."

"Now you know it wasn't a dream."

Christian nodded.

"There's a darkness here. I've felt it for a long time now. I've always felt in control of it. This is my hospital. My kingdom, and I know everyone and everything within it."

Kristin raised her arms slightly, and the cable ties around her wrists snapped away with ease.

"Not anymore you're not."

Christian pushed his chair back from the desk, slightly concerned, but when Kristin made no effort to get up or move towards him, he relaxed a little more.

"Don't worry Doc, I'm not gonna kill you. Yet."

He nodded warily.

"Good to know."

Now it was Kristin's turn to ask more questions.

"Why don't you tell me what happened with Angie."

Now Christian was worried.

"How do you know about Angie?" he said, a slight quiver in his voice.

Kristin kept her eyes locked on him.

"I saw her. And I saw what she did to you."

"But… how?"

Kristin wasn't sure she could answer that, but she gave it her best shot.

"Last year, I ended up somewhere I shouldn't have. A place where humans aren't supposed to go. I experienced a thousand lifetimes of death, pain, and suffering before an old friend set me free. But something changed in me. I keep seeing those memories on repeat. They flash over and over in my mind, building up the pain and the rage associated with it, and then… well you know what happens. Somehow, I'm evolving into something else. And whatever that thing is, it allowed me somehow to see into the past."

For the first time since Christian had met Kristin, he actually believed her. She had told the story of being tortured in a mystic place somewhere in another realm, but it was immediately put down to a mental illness, she was sectioned, and brought to Moriarty. But he could no longer deny what was happening here, and suddenly this story was entirely plausible.

He turned his chair around so he was facing the window, looking out into the tiny light of the early hours. The sun would soon be up. Another night gone without sleep. He closed his eyes and tried to access the memories that he had buried so long ago.

"I'd caught one of the guards with one of the patients one night on my way out. Apparently, it had been going on for a while. She was here under her family's request, extreme paranoia, so she was able to consent to a relationship. But the guard got mad, and lashed out at me. I was carrying my briefcase. I hit him in the side of the head and he went down. I didn't even hit him that hard. But it was done. He was dead. The patient lost it. Started screaming at the top of her lungs, and I… I couldn't think straight. I lunged towards her to try and silence her, but… I tripped over the guard on the floor, and fell into her. When I got up, I realised I'd pushed her into the stone wall behind her. I didn't even hear her head crack against it. I was just trapped in a nightmare."

Kristin finally broke her gaze. Something so simple, however inappropriate, and lives were ruined. Just like that. Christian continued.

"I was the only one on the wing at the time, everyone else had gone hours ago except for the night staff who were on the lower levels doing their rounds. I dragged their bodies down the hallway to my office. I can still hear the squeaking of the guard's leather belt and his shoes as they dragged along the tiles."

Whilst Christian wasn't inflicted with a visit to the home of the Pain Wraiths, he certainly inhabited a few similar memories. He was visibly altered by what had happened. Kristin listened as a few more blanks were filled in.

"When I got to my office, I called the only man I ever knew that I could trust implicitly."

"Kenrick."

He nodded.

"We'd enlisted with the marines when we were teenagers, but I didn't make the cut. Kenrick made his name as an interrogation specialist. He was sent in when information was needed, no questions asked. We kept in touch all that time. He was here within the hour. He took care of the bodies, told me to ask no questions.

The next day, I started hearing rumours that something had happened the previous night, and heard whispers of my name being mentioned. That's when I found out there was a witness."

Kristin recalled the name instantly.

"Naomi."

Christian looked over his shoulder at her, but the surprise at her knowing the details soon faded, and he looked at the floor and nodded, before swivelling back towards the window.

"She saw everything. She couldn't sleep and was looking through her door window opposite when it all happened. I called Kenrick and he told me what to do. I had her relocated to the far end of the hospital. We had nicer rooms down there. They used to be where kids could visit with their parents if they were ever admitted here. Brighter colours, big windows, less security precautions."

Now the wooden frame and open windows made sense. Kristin knew the rest of that part of the story.

"You had Kenrick interrogate her. And when she wouldn't give up what she saw, you had him kill her, and make it look like she broke out."

He nodded.

"They found her body with the cuts and tears from the glass in the woods behind the hospital three days later. By then the wolves had gotten to her and…"

He trailed off. And Kristin knew what came next.

"Your wife saw you didn't she?"

Again he nodded.

"She came to see if I wanted a late dinner on her way home from work, and was told where I was by reception. She saw the whole thing. When I tried to tell her that I was just trying to protect myself for our family's sake, she ran. She always carried a small knife for protection, but I never realised what a strange sensation being stabbed would be. At first it just felt hot, like a glancing brush against a stove. Then came the pain."

Christian instinctively raised his hand to his abdomen. He flinched at the memory of the pain despite there being no lasting discomfort.

"I used the last of my strength to pick up my phone and call Kenrick. He'd just finished dumping Naomi's body in the woods. I only meant for him to bring her back. She was never meant to get hurt."

Despite her new found inner strength, Kristin inhaled sharply, and placed her hand over her mouth.

"He killed her?" she asked.

Christian couldn't look at her. He simply nodded.

"He didn't know she was my wife. He thought she was another witness. She had a hospital admittance pass, and she'd kept her name when we got married. I saw it on the news the next day. A truck driver found her under a bridge on the interstate. One gunshot wound to the head. Gun was next to her on the pavement, with only her fingerprints. Ruled suicide."

Engrossed in the story, Kristin felt a little more uneasy than she had done since she entered the office. She tilted her head slightly, but heard no noise behind her. She couldn't explain it, but something just felt... off. Christian obviously didn't notice.

"The hardest part was Lucy."

"Lucy?"

"My daughter."

Kristin hadn't realised he had kids. He seemed like such a monster, it never even crossed his mind that he'd been married until she relived the memory of Naomi's demise.

"When she heard what happened to her Mom, she retreated into herself. Started using drugs, and drinking. I was never there for her. I was consumed by this place. Last time I saw her, she was packing her bags one morning. We just looked at each other, and I left for work. I never saw her again."

The air had definitely shifted. Something was wrong. Kristin's skin was beginning to itch, and she felt a cold shiver run up her back. It felt like some kind of withdrawal symptom. She had experienced it only once before. Years before she met Kathryn and the others, she had been involved with a bounty hunter, who liked to work hard and party harder. She would drag Kristin into every bar on the circuit, and Kristin became dependant on the alcohol. It took a lot for her to break away from that relationship and ditch the booze. It was probably why she felt so much anger towards Kathryn when she started drinking more and more over the last four years or so. Despite her problems, she had never quite managed to kick the booze altogether, but had gotten some kind of grasp on it.

Then she heard it.

A faint scream in the distance.

Then another.

This time, Christian heard it too.

"What was that?" he asked, swivelling round in his chair.

Kristin shook her head indicating she wasn't sure. She was experiencing discomfort herself and was once more finding it hard to focus. They both stood and moved towards the door. As they did so, a black shadow flashed across the doorway, and on the other side of the door, they heard multiple sickening crunches, and the sound of bodies hitting the floor. Kristin turned to Christian.

"I think it's safe to say we're on our own now."

A loud clunk echoed around the entire hospital, and the power went out.

They were now consumed by darkness.

FOURTEEN

The darkness actually seemed to help Kristin focus more than in the light. She felt as if the absence of brightness was now a comfort to her. Her mind felt the calmest it had in weeks, even more so than her earlier experience of briefly controlling her new found power. Christian, on the other hand, was not quite so calm.

As the two of them made their way out of the office, feeling along the wall, she could hear his breath getting faster and faster, and amongst the quiet in her head, his breaths were like an echo in an empty space.

"Will you please, shut the fuck up!" she whispered harshly.

"Forgive me if I'm a little paranoid that some vicious killer ghost is gonna eat me! And by the way, I'm not exactly feeling secure around you either!"

Kristin scoffed in his direction. She stumbled as her foot caught the now either unconscious, or dead body of one of the guards that had stood outside the door. She carefully walked around the body, and it was then that she had to stop and think.

Echoing around the hallways, the entire building in fact, were the distant sounds of screams. Terror. Some of them bloodcurdling. But her reason for hesitance was that she could not be certain these were not her own sounds and images trying to return to the front of her mind. There was only one way to know for sure. She turned around, and to her surprise, saw Christian as clearly as if it were day time, albeit with a photo negative vibe.

"Do you hear that?" she asked.

Christian clearly could not see her as clearly as she could see him, as his hands were still out in front of him. What she did spot though, was him slyly concealing the barrel of a gun into the back of his waistband.

"I'm trying not to," came his reply.

Well, at least she knew this was an external horror and not more internal trauma. While she was fairly sure she could take him down if the need arose, Kristin suggested Christian take the lead.

"Are you crazy?"

Kristin rolled her eyes at the ironic complaint.

"Fine, but try to keep up."

She moved further ahead of him to ensure some degree of safe distance. Either for her, or for him. A loud whooshing sound passed along the bottom of the hallway ahead of them. Kristin paused. More screams.

Then silence.

Christian bumped right into the back of Kristin, knocking her forwards into the opposite wall, where she hit her head. A surge of rage went through her, and she span and launched her hand into Christian's throat, lifted him clean off the floor, and pinned him there.

"Watch where you're going you little prick!"

Christian's left hand was reaching for his gun, but it was too far away. His face was contorted with fear, but Kristin was oblivious to the display of strength she was currently exhibiting. Her own face changed slightly, and appeared more confused.

"What? What is it?" she asked, more calmly, but still not releasing her grip.

"Y… your… eyes…"

That was all Christian could spit out between gasps for air, and it was only then that Kristin saw when she turned her head, two small dots of light appearing on surfaces opposite wherever she was looking. Whatever was inside her, had activated once again.

She looked back at the doctor still pinned to the wall, slowly losing consciousness, and while she knew she should let him down, part of her new personality wanted to see how long she could toy with him, and keep him suspended between life and death. Just like earlier, she felt a smile creep onto her face.

Christian was now just moments from death, his eyes began to roll back into his head, but from nowhere, the whooshing noise returned, and hit Kristin in the ribs like a freight train, and sent her flying acrobatically through the air at least thirty feet back past the office door, before smashing through a viewing window to the arts and crafts room, and landing on the other side in a collection of broken glass, and furniture.

Back down the corridor, Christian's coughs and splutters were now deafening against the previous silence as he tried to regain some kind of composure. Kristin, however, was now leaping to her feet, and sat hunched ready to strike. There was no pain in her body, her injuries were clear, but not causing discomfort. And she felt energised. It was as if she had been plugged into the mains, and she felt static running all along her skin.

"WHERE ARE YOU?" she bellowed out into the empty hallways.

More distant whooshing sounds, followed by individual screams this time. It would seem that whatever had made its way through the facility now only had bare bones of meat left to pick. As Kristin got up to her full height, she noticed there were also bodies dotted on the floor around her. The new found night vision she had seemingly developed, gave her a full view of the carnage and death.

She counted fifteen dead, all in various states of decay. This attack could not have happened more than fifteen minutes ago based on their conversation in the office, and yet some of these bodies seemed almost mummified, others nearly down to the bone. Ribcages were broken and protruding from the chest of one of the former nurses, hunched up against the wall. Another nurse was splayed on a table, their top half hanging over the edge at a perfect ninety degree angle. The man had been broken in half, with only his skin keeping him in one piece.

But the true horror here, was not that this macabre event had happened, but that as she gazed upon each drained or mutilated body, Kristin felt a growing hunger. These deaths were giving her *pleasure*.

"Kristin?" came the whimpering voice of Christian, still where she had dropped him.

Her head snapped back around, and she bared her teeth. The smile was now etched onto her face, and she bounded forward, leaping through the window, and making great strides down the hallway.

The sound of a gun cocking joined her footfalls, and as she pulled back an arm and prepared to strike, five shots rang out in quick succession. Each bullet stopped exactly one millimetre from her body. She came to a halt at the same time as the bullets, and she could feel a glow of energy around her body, her mind now using the painful memories as a generator once more, and her focus on the bullets was absolute. Each one was a separate image in her mind, and she one by one, in turn, altered the bullets' aim until each one was pointing back towards Christian.

And then she let them go.

The sound of the metal casing ripping through his flesh was almost as loud as the shots themselves had been. Each one fed Kristin with more endorphins, and she almost cackled as the fifth one tore through Christian's skull. The bone surface crunching under impact brought her such joy that she closed her eyes tightly.

But then, there was nothing.

No sound of a body hitting the floor, no sound of gargling blood.

Nothing.

She opened her eyes, and to her confusion, she saw Christian still slumped on the floor where she had left him, holding his neck, trying to catch his breath. She also felt weaker, more normal. Although her vision was still enhanced, and she was standing amongst broken glass, none of what she just saw had transpired.

"Ch.. Christian?" she asked into the darkness.

"Stay away from me!" he yelled back.

"Did you just shoot at me?" she asked, her voice getting more and more normal with each syllable.

"What? Why would I be on the floor trying to uncrush my windpipe if I'd shot you!"

She walked around the side of the broken window, and used the actual door to exit the arts room. As she approached Christian, he scrambled away, but she held her hand up in peace.

This of course was futile, and she forgot he couldn't see it, so accompanied it with 'wait'.

"We have a new problem," she said, looking all around them.

"And just what is that?" asked the doctor, still with a distinct rasp in his voice.

"Whatever this thing is… it can control my thoughts."

Christian let go of his neck and looked directly at Kristin's outline in the darkness.

"Wait, what?"

"It made me see an entire scenario that didn't happen. But that's not the worst part."

Christian was afraid to ask, but he did so anyway.

"Oh yeah? Then what's the worst part?"

Kristin grew another small grin.

"The worst part is… I liked it."

FIFTEEN

The ticking of the clock behind Frank Short's head was beginning to burrow into his skull like a drill. He had spent the last hour and a half trying to find out all he could about nearby facilities that specialised in one on one patient care. He had found none. He and his team had always had reservations surrounding Moriarty Hospital. For years there had been whisperings coming from within about experimental treatments, and failing standards. As for Doctor Christian Verne, Frank's digging had turned up some interesting information.

His phone screen lit up, and the device began to vibrate across his desk. Glancing at the screen, he saw Beth Ford's name. It had been almost a year since she transferred to Trinity Bay, and as yet Frank had not been assigned a new partner. Nobody had managed to fill the void. She was a hell of a cop.

"Long time no speak, Detective."

Giggling from the other end of the phone line made Frank smile.

"It's been long enough Frank. When are you and Amanda gonna come over here and have a drink with me? Dad keeps asking after you."

Frank's smile receded slightly at the sound of his wife's name. He had not yet told Beth that the pair had divorced. But that wasn't a conversation for now.

"Soon, I promise," he lied. "But I doubt you're calling me in the wee small hours of the morning for pleasantries, am I right?"

A brief silence filled the air, before Beth spoke again.

"Frank, I've had something very strange come across my desk during the night. I've got a lot of weird shit goin' on here. Hell, I'm starting to think that Trinity Bay might just be Wealdstone Mark II at this point. But in terms of conventional admin type stuff… this is weird."

Frank's curiosity was peaked. He reached behind his chair and grabbed the now luke-warm pot of coffee and began to pour a cup. Needless to say after almost twelve hours on the heat pad, it was more like caffeinated gravy.

"Well that makes two of us. You go first."

"Okay… I had an order come through to contact Moriarty Hospital, and demand the release of Kristin Silverton."

Now that made Frank sit up. Why would Beth have received the same order that he had? She wasn't in charge of the case, she was merely his partner. She was, however, now a fully fledged lead detective herself, so perhaps their mystery person thought she had sway now.

"Ditto."

Frank's reply was short but to the point.

"Yeah but you don't have the resources here that I do."

The smile returned to his face. The only benefit that Frank saw in his partner moving to Trinity Bay was the whole lack of jurisdiction. The freedom that it brings was tempting even to him, but it also had its issues.

"Go on then, tell me what my maverick ex-partner has dug up. Because I've got fuck all."

As if by magic, Frank's printer burst into life and began churning several pages towards him.

"I can hear that you still haven't changed your printer password, Frank."

He laughed, and took a sip of his coffee gravy.

"You took the damn manual with you, and you know me. I'm an analogue kinda guy."

"Yeah, I'm amazed you can work a smartphone without me. But seriously, take a look at who sent the request."

The printer stopped, and he pulled the papers out of the tray. Lifting them in front of his exhausted face, he squinted, but didn't need to do so for long. The picture on the front of the file was very clear.

"Are you sure?"

"100% positive."

"What the hell could they possibly want with Kristin Silverton?"

"I really don't wanna think about it. Whatever it is, they must have high backing, given their history. And what worries me, is that she isn't the first rumoured lunatic they've tried recruiting."

Frank turned the page, and there was indeed a list of former interests of the person in question.

"Jesus, they really are trying to build some sort of *Suicide Squad* for something."

He moved his finger down the list, absorbing every name on it.

Scarlett Fry

Samuel Greenwood

John Martin

Herman Fredericks

Tommy Frank

Kristin Silverton

Joshua Shaw

All of the names on the list of theorised targets were those of people either connected to Wealdstone, or Kristin herself. And all of them were now dead. Except for one.

"Who's Joshua Shaw?" Frank asked.

"As far as I can tell, nobody. According to my sources, they haven't actually contacted him yet. He's a former internet streamer, lost a lot during the whole exploding town scenario, now works at a soup kitchen, and writes comic books. Nothing significant. No priors, no criminal record to speak of. Never even dropped a piece of litter."

Frank went over the list once more.

"It's almost as if they knew these people were going to die. It's very strange. But what are they up to? I mean nobody has even seen this asshole in over a decade. Why now?"

Frank could hear Beth now crunching some kind of food on the other end of the phone, and moved the device away from his ear slightly.

"No idea. But they clearly have an agenda here. Frank, can I ask you something. And I'm being deadly serious here."

Frank paused as he raised his cup again.

"Sure. Anything."

Beth took a deep breath.

"Do you think any of this stuff is actually real? The werewolves attacking the Silverton District. The reports of mystical beings being involved in Wealdstone's decimation? What went down at Crossroads? I've seen things here, Frank. Things I can't explain. And I know you have seen things too."

Frank lowered his cup. He had thought about some of the things he had dismissed as impossible. The clearly bogus news reports, and suggestions of gas explosions, and any other excuse feasible enough to cover up an underlying truth. He remembered the CCTV footage of Kristin and what she did in the store where they found her. *Something* happened to her.

"I don't know, Beth. Too much is happening in this world now. And I'm out of ways to explain it. Something else has to be happening in these towns. And Doctor Verne is keeping something from me. I'm gonna pay him a little visit, I think."

Frank stood up, and grabbed his jacket from the back of his chair. He grabbed his cup and poured the thick dark liquid out the open window into the grass on the other side.

"Frank, do me a favour. There's a scientist I want you to take with you. She has only recently shown up on the radar. Probably because she's in Wealdstone, and we know how many things have happened there that we can't explain."

Frank laughed sarcastically.

"Yeah, you can say that again."

"I know, but I think she might be able to help. Her name is Chantel Beaufoy. She's got PhDs in Epidemiology, Molecular Medicine, Cybernetics, Genetics, Stem Cell Biology and Regenerative Medicine. If ever you need someone with their head screwed on to tell you if it's science, or actual evil magic, she's probably the one."

Frank glanced back up at the clock.

"Alright. Give her my number and tell her I'll pick her up at Deanna's Place in two hours. I'm gonna need some breakfast pie."

He said his goodbyes, and ended the call, sliding the phone into his jacket pocket. As he moved to walk out of his office, he stopped and picked up the file Beth had sent over. Something about this seemed off to him, and more than just bribing government officials to get this release order. But right now, he had to focus on his current task.

He threw the file back down on the desk, and switched out the lights. The little green blinking light on his printer allowed just enough illumination to highlight the company name on the top of the report.

H. J. Enterprises.

SIXTEEN

Caution was now just a distant memory for Kristin. Despite the fact that she had a formerly obsessive doctor with a firearm behind her, an unknown violent entity hunting her down, and her own emerging bloodlust, she needed to find the answers to all of this. In that respect, she finally understood Christian's aggressive stance. He had been blinded by fear, and it had cost him everything but his reputation. And now even that would be destroyed. The amount of deaths in the hospital had already sealed his doom.

It had been over an hour since Kristin's vision of her killing Christian, and she had tried to push it to the back of her mind as they had made their way around the facility. So far, they had come across at least seventy bodies in various states of mutilation, decomposition, and others simply frozen in fear on the floor. Against Christian's suggestion, they had been slowly descending into the lower levels of the hospital.

The whirring in her head was beginning to spin with such strength that once again she felt herself charging. Part of her thought process as they stepped over the bloodied corpses was to examine each one. She couldn't explain it, but the more death she saw, the more of a dopamine rush it gave her. Whilst she was in control of herself, she could continue. But she was concerned about the ease at which this entity could project imagery into her mind. It was almost like being subjected to the similar conditions of the Realm of Screams. The only difference was this time, she felt pleasure instead of pain.

"For the last time, why the hell are we going down?"

Christian's voice penetrated the silence and there was still a distinct rasp in his voice. Clearly the force Kristin had applied to his throat was having a lasting effect.

Another shot of dopamine.

"Because we need to seek this thing out, and I can feel us getting closer."

The pale light from a torch Christian had found on one of the dead guards was now beginning to flicker. To be honest, he wondered if he would prefer going back into the darkness. There was so much death. Never before, even in his worst nightmares had he encountered such cruelty and evil. And he had done some things that would certainly have fallen into those categories. Kenrick's arrival was a good example of that. And Angie of course.

But all of that bravado was gone. Every single last ounce of it. The Christian Verne now seeking out some paranormal force with a potentially possessed demon was nothing but a broken quivering wreck.

A loud bang came from directly ahead, and the two of them instinctively hunkered down. Christian pointed his failing flashlight towards the sound, and just caught the tail end of what looked to be a swirling mass vanishing around the next corner. As he moved the light down, its beam caught a leg.

Without the rest of the body.

"It's getting stronger," Kristin offered.

"And you still want to hunt it down?" Christian replied.

"Yes. I… I *feel* it. It's speaking to me. I can't explain it."

Another noise as they reached the corner, and this time, the flashlight caught more. The swirls of black and teal strands intertwined with each other in such a rapid motion, the image appeared to be playing out at double speed. But something was different.

The mass was beginning to form a more humanoid shape.

Kristin watched on, slowly advancing, as the strands of shiny material carefully began to construct a body. It appeared to be the back of a person. Hair began to form, and the figure twitched to the side as a loud crunching of bone could be heard. There were more jerky movements, and more crunches. Looking down at the creature's base, blood began to pool.

Christian moved forward, but his foot kicked a discarded beaker, sending it clattering into the opposite wall. The creature snapped around, the mimicked head seeming to swivel three-hundred-sixty degrees without the body moving. A black hole where a mouth should be opened wider than any human could manage, and it let out a demonic shriek.

Christian replied in his own cry of terror, and bolted in the opposite direction, leaving Kristin dead centre as the entity morphed into its usual state and launched forwards like a torpedo. As it hit Kristin, it struck her in the chest, forcing her to double over, but it blew through her, twisting and sliding around her bones, organs and flesh, and burst out of her back as if she were a ghost. It vanished into the distance chasing after Christian, but the effect it had had on Kristen was powerful.

She dropped to her knees, and she could see her skin beginning to bubble. The ripples continued all over her body. Tearing open the top of her vest top, she could see bubbles making their way along her collarbone, and felt them rising up her neck. When they reached her head, she threw herself back onto the cold floor, her eyes burned violet, and she let out a roar of anger so loud, the nearby windows within each cell door, exploded outwards, raining shards of glass all over her. She twisted her head left and right at such speed, it was almost at a literal breakneck level. Her fists pounded the tiles either side of her, until they shattered.

And then it was gone.

As quickly as the phenomenon had burst through her body, it had dissipated. But Kristin had never felt such a rush. It was as if the creature, or entity, or whatever this thing was, existed because of pure pain, and its contact with Kristin in her evolving state was providing extreme pleasure to her in every way. She was once again in control of her functions, but her desire for more of this feeling was now almost insatiable. She scrambled to her feet, and charged off down the hallway manically looking for the source of this.

She wondered if it had caught up with Christian yet, but her concern was not that he was still alive. It was that she might have missed his suffering.

SEVENTEEN

"So how did you get involved with Kristin?"

Chantel's question kind of caught Frank off guard. He had actually been in or around Kristin for several years, and the more this case made him think about it, the more he began to realise perhaps he had seen even more than his eyes had led him to believe.

"Well, I was involved with the opening of that eyesore she built when I was a uniform cop. She barely acknowledged our existence. Too busy staring down the locals who were protesting the place. Then a few more times before I transferred out of Wealdstone, and in the end, I was the one who arrested her when she finally got carted away last year."

Chantel nodded, all the time typing things into her laptop.

"How about you? We don't have a lot of info on you Dr Beaufoy. How long have you been involved with her?"

Chantel smiled, and closed her laptop lid.

"I'm involved with her niece."

"Ah."

Frank was always uncomfortable around people from the LGBTQ+ community. He admired their strength and courage and their ability to keep pushing for equality, but being one of what many people would call the 'Old Guard', he was always worried about misgendering or misidentifying someone, and so tended to skirt around the subject.

"Don't worry, Detective. My uncle was the same. You offend people more by ignoring them, so don't worry about offending people. If your intentions are good, they will correct you and help you through it."

What had just happened? Did she read my thoughts, he thought? Either way, he felt more at ease already.

"But to elaborate, I met Grace in Paris. We had a little bit of… trouble there, and I ended up in Crossroads. I'm sure you heard about what happened there."

He certainly had. He didn't realise Chantel had been present at Crossroads. He had so many questions, but the journey to the hospital was at least another hour long and he needed to fill that time somehow.

"Don't take offence, Doctor Beaufoy, but you don't exactly look like a scientist."

She looked directly at him, and he immediately feared he had offended her, but she began to smile.

"I think that's one of the nicest things anyone has ever said to me."

A little disarmed, but happy nonetheless, Frank smiled himself.

"Sorry, it sounded negative, but you just look more like a biker chick than a squint."

Chantel laughed out loud, and it was infectious. Frank joined the laughter, but he was confused.

"What?" he asked between laughs.

"You do know we had *Bones* in France right? The squints were one of the best parts. You literally just gave me a huge compliment and then took it away. I can be a biker chick squint, it is the 2020's."

The next twenty minutes or so of the journey went in a similarly upbeat way, until they came to discussing the details of this particular issue.

"So I've looked over the files your partner sent me, and I'm beginning to piece together an idea of what H.J. Enterprises are up to."

That wasn't the first thing that came to his mind, though. She had just breezed past the whole Kristin case file. He held up his hand to stop her.

"That wasn't the part I needed help with Doctor. I need to know your opinion on Kristin herself."

This is where Chantel's demeanour changed. It was as if she was weighing up whether or not to say something. The next question made him realise his original line of thinking may be correct after all.

"Have you seen something, Detective, that you can't explain? Or something that can only truly be explained by being supernatural?"

Frank gripped the wheel tightly. He had. On multiple occasions. Once more, his mind went back to how quickly he saw Kristin snap into ninja mode on the camera footage.

"Yes."

Chantel appeared to relax slightly, took a deep breath and began.

"I'm going to tell you something now, and I need to you to know that I'm not crazy. I've had a year or so to process it, so I need you to keep an open mind."

"I'm all ears."

Chantel put her laptop in the footwell and stared directly out the window at the passing lines in the road under the beams of the headlights.

"I'm not from your reality."

She looked over to Frank, but his face remained unchanged. So she continued.

"I was living in a post-apocalyptic Paris where the undead had taken over the world, and I had been working for several years on a cure. And I found one. The problem was, there was something far worse out there."

Surprisingly, Frank's reply caught her completely unawares.

"Monarch."

"How… I thought that whole thing was covered up? How could you possibly know…"

Frank held up his hand.

"My wife. She went to visit her sister in Wealdstone one weekend. She didn't come home. I was so wrapped up in work that I didn't think too much of it. I was never exactly her sister's first choice for Amanda. Turns out, she was one of the people Monarch coerced into moving to that shithole Crossroads."

It appeared that Chantel was correct in being able to trust Frank with the truth. He had a deeper involvement with all this than she could ever have realised. In fact, she got the distinct impression that he had tried to rationalise and compartmentalise all of his experiences to ignore the truth. Perhaps he finally realised that he could hide the facts no longer.

"Did she…"

He nodded.

"Yeah she got out of there. Made her way home, but she was never the same. After about 3 months, we knew the marriage was over. The things she had seen, and my inability to comprehend any of it just drove us apart. Six months after the whole event, we were divorced. Twenty-four years of marriage, destroyed by something she described as a Yellow Demon."

That phrase got her attention.

"Would it help you to know she was right?"

She thought she saw a tiny tear forming in the corner of Frank's eye. In the short time she had been with him, she had managed to deduce he was regretful of the break down of his marriage due to things he couldn't process at the time.

"I often wonder if it had all happened just a year later and I was more open minded, as I am having to be now, whether we would still be together. But it's too late now."

Chantel, instinctively placed a hand on his arm in an effort to comfort him. He nodded slightly in recognition of the attempt. Chantel leaned forward and picked up her laptop, opening it to the file she had been examining.

"You know, I didn't know Kristin for very long. Literally a matter of hours. Her friends and Grace all tell me she was the heart of their little team until her and Kathryn drifted apart. But from what I saw personally, she is dangerous, manipulative and untrustworthy. I learned since then that she experienced a thousand lifetimes of torture leading up to those events at Crossroads, but there is no way something like that allows you to go back to who you were. She is different now. And I hope your mind remains open Detective, because something is happening to Kristin. Something otherworldly."

EIGHTEEN

The mirrors were like a tunnel of eternity. Each one reflected the one behind it over and over again, with Kristin's body stuck in the middle. This was a part of the hospital she had never been in before. It was some sort of storage space between floors, and lining both sides of the walls were full length mirrors, presumably left over from the infrequent refurbishment of the shower or toilet blocks. Kristin had only entered this area after hearing scuttling in the dark. She presumed in a building of this age and disrepair, it was simply rats or a raccoon. But given her current circumstances, she suspected it could be more. Maybe a mortally wounded doctor cowering in a corner bleeding to death.

She hoped.

As powerful as she was feeling inside, she was not prepared for what came next. She glanced into one of the mirrors, and she fell to the ground, open mouthed at what she saw.

Reflected in the mirror, was not the image of her own presence, but six individual nooses, hanging from the beyond the top of the mirror somewhere. In each of those nooses was the decomposing body of someone she knew.

In the first noose was Kathryn. Her neck was clearly broken, and the bruising ran up the right side of her neck. In the second, was Daniella. That one hit harder than she expected. After all, she had no idea if Daniella was dead or alive following her disappearance. The third one caused her to gasp out loud. Grace's body seemed like it had been stretched from the neck. The rope had sliced into the skin, and become soaked in her blood. The skin surrounding the neck appeared to have fallen victim to slippage, giving the illusion that her neck was longer than it was. In noose number four, she saw Annie. A thin blue vapour floated around her body. Her hair was matted to her face, and her cheekbones were visible through the shrinkage of her skin on her face. Number five was occupied by Deanna. She had found it difficult to get over her death at the hands of Jasmine, and seeing her now brought it all rushing back to the surface. And finally, Duncan's lifeless body occupied the final hanging place. His chest had been cut open, and his blood continued to drip to the floor. The sound of the crimson fluid bouncing on the tiled floor echoed around the empty space.

And then she saw it.

Movement behind the bodies of her friends and family.

The glint of a blade caught her eye.

"No… it can't…"

A mirror image of Kristin stepped out from behind Kathryn's body, twirling a small, narrow blade in her hand. Her eyes were glowing violet, but her mouth was surrounded by decay. Black thin lines cracked their way from her lips which were grey and hardened, along the veins beneath her face, fading out as they reached her nose, and chin in opposite directions. The image glared back at Kristin and her mouth widened into a devilish grimace. Black fluid spilled from her open mouth and ran down her chin onto her shirt.

"You…. You caused this. You caused it all!"

Kristin threw herself backwards as the mirror image launched at her in the reflection, and her back broke through the mirrors on the opposite side. The mirror in which she had been staring exploded outwards, and she attempted to shield herself from the shards to no avail. One by one, the larger shards sliced through her skin like scissors nipping at each point. The smaller pieces pierced her skin like brushing thorns on a cactus, and she could feel trickles of blood running down various points of her skin.

One by one, the mirrors along the crawlspace blew apart, the tinkling of the shattered glass raining down onto the floor. As the final mirrors crashed into pieces, there was a brief silence. Then, suddenly, all of the broken glass lifted from the floor where that last mirror had stood. It rose and fell like a wave, moving towards Kristin at pace. She wanted to move, but she couldn't. She closed her eyes, and felt the generator of images spinning out of control. They were all a blur now. She tensed her muscles until they hurt and veins began popping along her skin, before throwing out her arms to her side.

An enormous purple bolt of energy exploded from her chest and blasted through the shards of glass. They parted and began to crumble to dust, but as Kristin let out a roar of hatred from her throat, the beam of energy blew through the end wall of the storage space, and kept going.

One by one, walls were destroyed, the bricks crumbling, any furniture in the way was obliterated, and the bodies of those who had been slain were disintegrated.

And then it stopped.

Kristin tried to catch her breath, panting heavily, but also between gasps for breath, she let out little giggles. The endorphins were back, and she was struggling to contain her glee. The power surging through her was intoxicating, better than any alcohol, or drugs. She had never felt more alive.

A cold, chilled breath formed on her neck, but rather than feel frightened, she felt aroused by it. Her eyes moved to the side seductively, and she felt the entity beside her. It whispered into her ear.

"You are ready, Kristin. The hurt and pain you have been subjected to has only helped to feed you. Use the pain. Let it replenish you…"

Kristin's smile spread wider and wider, until drool began to fall from her mouth, similar to the horrifying image she had witnessed moments ago.

"Join with me, Kristin. We can take revenge on them all."

The black and turquoise mixture began to wrap itself around Kristin's arms and legs, and it felt like the touch of a lover caressing her skin. Her eyes closed gently, and she began to inhale deeply.

"KRISTIN DON'T DO IT!"

Christian's voice bellowed through the newly created tunnel, and the entity immediately began to recede from her body. Christian aimed his gun at the mass, knowing it wouldn't make a difference, but he fired the shots anyway. Each one was absorbed, and fell to the floor. The creature let out a deafening shriek and burst forward. Christian dived to the left, but that was not solid ground. He tumbled down a small flight of stairs, and managed to look back just as the entity ploughed through the solid wall that had been behind him, and vanished.

Wincing in pain, and cradling his shoulder, he dragged himself to his feet, and lumbered back up the few stairs, where he saw Kristin had not moved. She looked slightly more normal than she had done moments before, and was aware of herself enough to look at him.

"Kristin, are you okay?" he asked tentatively.

She said nothing for a moment.

"Why?"

Christian was waiting for more, but it didn't come. She simply repeated the same question, and appeared to be in pain.

"Why?"

Christian moved forward slightly.

"Why what? Why did I stop it?"

Kristin now began to clench her jaw.

"I felt so… content. Now I just feel… broken again."

He noticed her fists beginning to clench up, and so stopped his advance.

"Kristin, whatever this thing is, it wants you specifically. Whatever is happening to you, it needs something from you. Why else would it be trying to merge with you?"

Kristin let out a deranged, maniacal laugh. It was something that greatly disturbed him. It was a laugh he had heard many, many times throughout his years in this institution.

It was the laugh of a mad woman.

"And who is she to you, Christian?" she spat accusingly.

"I don't…"

"YOU DON'T WHAT?!" she bellowed.

Christian began to back up as she moved towards him, stomping her feet in the dust that used to be glass.

"YOU DON'T WANT TO ADMIT IT, DO YOU?"

Her voice seemed to be growing louder with each syllable. But then it dropped and her head tilted sharply to the side.

"Yes, there is a link there. It… no… *she* wants something. Something from us both… why aren't you dead yet? I don't know. Do you know? No, I don't know either. She wants something… needs it"

Christian almost felt sorry for her. She had finally broken. Her mind had finally given up, and now any control she had over herself was gone. He still cradled the gun in his hand. One shot left.

"Kristin, I think you need to let me get you some help. You're becoming crazy and…"

"SAY THAT AGAIN, I DIDN'T QUITE HEAR YOU!"

This time, the bellowing voice created a shockwave, and physically knocked him down onto his backside, the gun bouncing down the stairs he had fallen down just minutes before.

Kristin stomped forward until she was standing directly over him, and she looked down, arms wide, fingers bent into crooked shapes, and her smile was fluctuating, her eyes flicking back and forth as if trying to find some kind of focus.

"Kristin, whatever it's doing to you, you need to fight it! It's killed and slaughtered its way through the hospital, and now it wants you too! We have to leave!"

She slowly knelt down next to him, and mimicked the face of someone thinking an option over. There was no acceptance in her eyes of his suggestion, she was mocking him.

"Or… and hear me out here… I could kill you and go and find her myself."

Christian began to slide away from her along the floor, but his shoulder was too injured to move quickly enough. Kristin raised her left leg, and brought it down on his shin with such force that his leg snapped in two. His cries bounced off every wall in the building, and a rush of pleasure burst through her veins.

A second stomp, and this time his right arm was the victim. He leaned over slightly and a projectile stream of vomit burst from his mouth, and began dripping down the stairs.

"Kris… Kristin… please, don't…"

Those were the last words Doctor Christian Verne ever uttered.

Each hammer of Kristin's foot crunched more and more bone away from the structure of his skull. First his nose broke free and blood flowed like a waterfall. Then the top of his skull caved. By the seventeenth blow, nothing remained that resembled a human head.

NINETEEN

"Shit."

The single word response from Frank was pretty much exactly the response Chantel had expected. During their dash towards Moriarty Hospital, she had furnished him with the true events of Crossroads, and while had had suspected there was more to what was reported, to now have that confirmed was on another level.

"Yeah. It's part of the reason Kathryn and Jack left Wealdstone. They couldn't get away from it all long enough to figure out what they wanted to do. Kristin was always sort of hanging around in the background whether physically there or not."

So many things now made a lot more sense. Frank understood how Kristin had gone so quickly from what she was to where she was now. She was not insane. At least not yet. But if Christian Verne had his way, she soon may be. What she needed was help, not persecution.

"So what did you and your partner find out about Doctor Verne?" Chantel asked.

Frank took a sip from his latte cup, and placed it back in the cupholder. The cardboard immediately stuck to the sticky plastic, an indication of the amount of coffees he had indulged in over the years.

"He was handed the reigns of Moriarty fifteen years ago, after impressing in a very specific kind of research. He had been working on a new way to stabilise people's minds through an intravenous drug, to help them achieve a more stable mind."

Chantel nodded. She was impressed.

"That's quite an achievement. Although, did it actually work?"

Frank slowly shook his head.

"Nope. He administered the drug to fifty people with the most severe paranoia and dementia, and for a year, they functioned almost as normal members of the community. Until they didn't."

"What happened?"

Frank raised his eyebrows. The details of these events always made him uncomfortable. His father had developed dementia before he died, and it terrified him to think this could have happened to him.

"Every single one of them went berserk and killed someone. The level of violence was that intense, most of them were taken down in police shootouts."

"Merde."

The pair sat in silence for a moment, to allow Chantel to digest the information. Clearly it hadn't changed people's minds about the good doctor, as he was still where he had been placed.

"Yeah. But never once did the board of directors for the hospital, government or anyone else question his integrity. They'd already invested too much money into his programs and into getting him into Moriarty. Its reputation was below rock bottom, so there was no way they were gonna allow some kind of media circus after such a quick appointment."

Chantel thought about something she had seen in the files that Beth Ford had sent over. She once again opened her laptop screen and began clicking away to traverse the vast data, until she found what she had been looking for.

"Wait, so H.J. Enterprises went dormant fourteen years ago?"

Frank nodded.

"And Doctor Christian got his position *fifteen* years ago."

More cautiously this time, Frank nodded again.

"And suddenly, H.J. Enterprises is seeking out people again? Curious. Has Christian Verne made any breakthroughs lately?"

Frank hadn't really thought too much about his recent history. He specialised in digging up the dirt in case he needed to use it to his advantage.

"Not that I know of. A couple of years ago, he did suddenly request a boost in funding, but it was rejected. The results in progress for the patients at Moriarty had nosedived. He had requested more resources be diverted to the care of patient…"

"47."

Chantel interrupted as the details came up on a file she really should not have been able to access.

"How did you get access to that?" Frank asked, suspecting he already knew the source.

Chantel smiled.

"You have a very resourceful partner, Detective Short."

"Mmhmm."

"These reasons he cited for the resources are very interesting. Increased mental acuity observed. Displays of seemingly exponential strength. Memory loss is an issue, but request for intense treatments and adjustments to facility are now an urgent requirement."

Frank turned off the highway onto the long straight road towards the facility. The building loomed on the horizon, and instantly gave Frank the chills. He did not enjoy the few times he had visited Moriarty in the past, and was not exactly eager to enter the perimeter once again.

"Yeah, I never found out who that patient was, but the funding was denied and the resources remained where they were."

Chantel scoffed. Frank looked at her with a puzzled face.

"What? Did I miss something?"

Chantel scoffed again.

"Yeah. A pretty fucking obvious thing! You are a detective right?"

"Hey! Easy there!"

Chantel held her hand up in apology.

"Heightened strength. Increased neural activity. Patient 47 is Kristin!"

Frank slammed the brakes, and Chantel lurched forwards, almost hitting her head on the dashboard. The dust on the road slowly settled behind them having been thrust into the air.

"Qu'est-ce que tu fous, Frank?! "

Frank turned and looked at her, no hint of an apology in his thoughts. Despite clearly missing the link between Patient 47 and Kristin, all of the information had been slowly trickling into the filing cabinet of his mind.

"I'm such an idiot!"

Chantel, now able to focus on her English again was confused.

"What, the 47 thing? It's okay, you know now."

Frank waved his hands frantically.

"No not that! H.J. Enterprises went dormant because people were starting to look into their activities a bit too closely. Then, Christian Verne turns up, with a huge amount of pomp and achievement behind him, and almost instant results."

Chantel's mind began to follow what he was getting at, but did not wish to interrupt him now he was in full flow.

"Don't you see? H.J. Enterprises *IS* Christian Verne! He's using Moriarty to further his experiments!"

Without waiting for a response from his passenger, Frank grabbed his radio from the dashboard.

"Dispatch this is 22-705, I need a 10-59 on a Doctor Christian Verne ASAP please. Suspected misdemeanour."

"Confirmed 22-705."

The radio fell silent for a few moments, before crackling back into life.

"Dispatch to 22-705. Dr Christian Verne. No priors, record is clean. However no detailed records exist beyond fifteen years ago. Request further action."

Frank and Chantel looked at each other, and the next step was clear. They needed to get in there and get in there now.

"Dispatch, this is 22-705. We have multiple 10-54s. Request armed backup to Moriarty Hospital immediately. 22-705 and 1 civilian on scene."

Chantel nudged Frank.

"What is a 10-54?"

"Possible dead body."

"Merde."

Frank nodded.

"22-705 this is Dispatch. Multiple units are en route to your location. Proceed with caution. Ambulance units also heading your way."

"22-705 all received."

Frank slammed the radio back into its holder, and planted his foot on the accelerator. The car burst forward and kicked up such a dust cloud from the tyres that the car and the facility were briefly hidden.

He had no idea what they were walking into, but he knew it was not going to be pleasant.

TWENTY

Kristin was now stumbling her way down the final corridor on the base level of the building. Her vision was blurred and distorted, and her muscles were now in agony from being tensed for so long. Every few steps, she slammed her fists into the side of her head trying to force her eyes to work as they should. She couldn't figure out what was real and what was an illusion anymore.

The image of Christian's crushed skull and brain matter dripping from her shoes was dominant in her frontal lobe, but she also had an image alongside it, of her looking back up the stairs to see no body at all. Did she kill him? Was it another invasion of her mind by this malicious entity?

"No… no… no… no… he's dead. I'm glad…. No, he's not dead… yes he is… no…"

Her ramblings were having less and less grip on the real world. The remaining strands of her sanity were letting go of the ball of string and she could feel herself pining for the strength the entity unlocked within her. She felt calm, and collected, and strong when it touched her.

She longed for that connection once more.

"Kristin."

She stopped dead.

Stood in front of her was what resembled a woman. But it wasn't a woman. It was the twisting tendrils of the malevolent presence that haunted this place. But it seemed to be more composed than she had seen it yet. It even appeared to be mimicking facial features.

"Who... what... are you?" Kristin asked between gasped breaths.

The woman seemed to float forwards, strands of her construction grasping the tiles and pulling her forwards without effort. The closer she got to Kristin, the clearer it was that the teal coloured accent to the black mass she had seen was that of a long dress. It was intertwined with the oily construction, but was the only real part of this... woman, that was clear.

"I've been waiting for you."

The air began to swirl around them both, and the tiny hairs on the back of Kristin's neck began to stand on end. The closer this creature got to her, the calmer her mind started to become. It was like a flashlight searching through the fog. As long as she stood in the beam of light, she was safe. Her own legs began to carry her towards the woman's figure. The brutal imagery of pain and death and the horrifying experiences she had gone through in the Realm of Screams was still inside of her, but the presence of whatever this creature was, had an addictive manipulation to it.

The sly smile began to spread across her face once more as they both reached within inches of each other.

"Kristin… you mustn't let him take you."

The unusual sentence broke Kristin's focus for a moment, and her eyes which had begun to close, immediately snapped open.

"What?"

The gradient strands of the woman's figure began to knit together more closely, until Kristin finally found herself staring at a fully formed woman. A woman she recognised.

"Don't let him take you too, Kristin. You have to stop him."

Kristin was staring at Angela Verne.

TWENTY ONE

There was a bright flash of light, and Kristin attempted to shield her eyes. As the light subsided, she could hear birdsong above her. Lowering her hands, she found herself standing near the gate to a children's play area. All around her people were smiling and enjoying the beautiful sunshine of the day. And stood next to her, was Angie. She was the only person to look out of place. Her dark tattered teal dress, matted with blood, and who knows what else. It only took a moment for Kristin to realise this was not real.

"Where are we?" she asked.

Angie pointed to a little girl who was currently bouncing up and down on a small trampoline.

"Do you see that little girl there?" she asked.

Kristin nodded.

"That is my daughter, Lucy."

Kristin remembered what Christian had said about Lucy. He had told her how she had turned to drink and drugs to cope with her mother's death before she disappeared.

Something about Angie's dead eyes suddenly became emotive and she felt that she had not been told the truth.

"What happened?"

"This was the day that I met him."

Kristin was now more confused than ever.

"Met who? I thought Lucy was your daughter with Christian?"

The clouds suddenly darkened, and the wind began to howl, and Kristin struggled to remain on her feet as the scene changed once again, and she was now on a boat at sea, standing towards the bow of the ship looking back in the direction of the pool.

She could see Christian with a little girl, possibly a slightly older Lucy, and they were seemingly struggling.

"This was the first time he hurt her."

Angie's voice was cold and fractious. Kristin watched on as Christian reached into his pocket and pulled out what looked like a needle. He yanked at the string holding the young Lucy's bikini pants on, pulled them aside and jabbed the needle into the flesh beneath the garment, before quickly putting it back in his pocket and tying up the bikini once more.

"What the fuck did he just do to her?" Kristin asked, feeling the anger rising within her.

"He was always obsessed with his work. We were just… patients in his grand scheme."

Again a sudden shift in weather conditions and the scene changed to a third visage. They were now standing in a warehouse of some kind. Kristin recognised it, she had hunted a clan of vampires in this very building not long after her encounter with the Sapphire Serpent. She was in Wealdstone. There were no vampires here though. This building was almost completely industrialised.

There were conveyor belts, and scientific equipment dotted everywhere, a few people in white lab coats, and then she saw him. Christian was standing over a girl, strapped to a table. The girl was now a young woman, Kristin guessed around sixteen years of age. She was overheating and sweating profusely. Kristin looked up and saw an intravenous bag hanging next to her filled with an orange liquid. The same orange liquid she had been administered twice. The girl was now in convulsions, and her wrists were straining against the straps holding her down.

"He used that drug on me. What is it?"

Angie struggled to contain her powerful rage, and Kristin began to feel it too, as if the two women were linked telepathically.

"He had been experimenting on women for over a decade when I met him. I just didn't know. Or didn't ask. I find it hard to remember the less clear memories. He told me she was sick. That he could help her."

Another jolt, another new image. This time, they were in a car park outside of a police station that she didn't recognise. Christian was arguing with the version of Angie that she had seen in the first memory in the hospital.

"I can't do that Angie! I won't let them stop my work, it's too important!" Christian yelled.

"You can't do this forever, Henry. One day you're going to kill someone, and they won't be able to save you from prison then. And where will your family be?"

"Henry?" Kristin's question of the name was muffled, and she watched as the argument escalated.

"My family? You are my wife, Angie. That girl is NOT my daughter. She had her chance to prove herself in my work, my medicinal advancements, but she left. As far as I'm concerned, she can rot in that jail cell!"

Christian, or Henry as Angie had called him, stormed off towards a nearby car, Angie following, her heels clacking hard on the tarmac.

"Angie, what's going on?"

"I found out what he was doing to Lucy, he confronted me, she hit him over the head with a tire iron, and then he had her arrested."

Kristin's mouth fell open with shock.

"You mean, they believed he was innocent?"

Angie nodded.

"He had given so many backhanders and bribes to bypass regulations and state requirements for medical licenses, that they just let him slide."

Kristin paused for a moment.

"Angie, you called him Henry."

Angie nodded.

"That is his real name. He changed it when H.J. Enterprises started getting investigated. Christian was what he chose in the end, but it never felt right."

Another jolt to the senses. This travelling through memories was beginning to make Kristin nauseous, even though she was acutely aware that she may not be in her own body right now.

This time, she was standing in a house, it was night, the clock on the wall said eight-thirty-five. Christian was standing next to the dining room table, looking down with rage, grasping a candlestick holder and breathing heavily. On the floor at his feet, was Angie.

"This was the night he forced me to take the new surname. I told him no, but by that point he had grown too powerful. He didn't hit me with the candle holder, he just threatened me with it, but it had the same effect. I agreed. The next day, we were out of there and on our way to Wellsfield."

That name rang a bell. That was where Kristin had suffered one of her very first blackouts. Had she truly travelled such a short distance in the year she had been away from Wealdstone?

"What about Lucy?" she managed to enquire.

"She was upstairs. Henry… Christian decided to drop the charges if I did what he told me. So I did."

Time rushed by, but this time, Kristin could see images. Familiar ones, very similar to the slideshow she was used to seeing in her head of death and violence, but this time it was people that Christian had tried to recruit for his experiments.

She saw the killer who had tried to murder Kristin, John Martin. Then an image of the detective that Ariella had been inhabiting, Sam Greenwood.

Scarlett. What could he possibly have wanted with Scarlett? Perhaps she had something within her even in this realm. The old man who followed she did not know, but recognised him from Annie's descriptions. Herman was opening his shop in the image she saw, with Christian standing outside the *Starbucks* opposite staring at him.

Then there was a young guy she didn't know. Curly hair, fluffy beard, serving soup to a bunch of people in a community hall of some kind. Christian was sat at one of the tables, looking roughed up to blend in. The final image was of Tommy, the guy who had taken Monarch's physical form out in the battle at Crossroads, but in this picture, he was strolling down Main Street in Wealdstone.

And then she saw herself. Not just once, but several times.

"Wh… what is this?"

"These are all the people you have encountered in your life, that he has tried to manipulate into joining his cause one way or another. You just didn't know it."

She saw him sitting on a park bench outside the café she met Kathryn at for their first financial advisor meeting about the museum. He was tying up a boat at the dock in Barbados when she went on the expedition to find the gold of the Sapphire Serpent. Again, on her honeymoon as her and Kathryn strolled along the beach. But why?

The clouds circled them both again, and now she was standing in Wellsfield General Hospital. She saw Christian talking to the doctors and she saw herself strapped to a hospital bed, eyes bright red, face soaked with tears, and the most vacant look she had ever seen. She knew when this was, however. This was after the inferno at the convenience store. She had been told about that day, but couldn't remember any of it. She tried to block the horror of her actions out but there had been too many incidents since then that were now a part of her.

"And this was the day he finally got his chance. He convinced the doctors to sign you over. Well, that and the crooked cop over there."

Christian was indeed looking over some paperwork with an older looking detective. She saw a slight of hand between the pair and a flash of green, before the detective nodded and walked away.

The imagery faded away, and the feelings of immense confusion began to drip back into Kristin's mind like a broken tap. She found herself standing back in the darkened hospital corridor at Moriarty, in front of Angie.

"Why did you show me all of that? He's dead, I killed him. This is all over now!" she bellowed, on the verge of tears.

Angie's figure began to twist and fade away again, but she saw a distinctive head shake.

"No, Kristin… he isn't. He's in your mind. Don't let him take you."

Flashes of violet light penetrated Kristin's vision, blinding her momentarily. When she finally got her eyes fully open, Angie's figure was gone, and Kristin was standing alone.

"He's in my mind… my mind… not dead…"

Her head flicked back and forth rapidly trying to make sense of everything. One minute she was calm and scared, the next she was angry and channelling Pain Wraith energy. What was real? What wasn't?

"Kristin? Are you okay?"

The sound of the voice made her jump. When she turned around, she saw Christian standing behind her, holding his hands up in peace.

"But… you… I… I killed you."

A confused look spread across his face, before he ran his hands over his own body.

"I'm pretty confident I'm still here."

His demeanour was different. He seemed cockier, more confident. Much more like she had seen him when she was placed on the table the first time.

"But… but… I remember… I think. Angie! I know about Angie and… Lucy!"

Christian began to laugh, much to Kristin's discomfort. He slowly stepped forward as he spoke.

"Of course you do, I told you all about them."

Kristin backed away, and she felt her rage building once more.

"No, I know you were experimenting on people… threatening your wife… you weren't Lucy's father…"

No reaction appeared on Christian's face.

"I have a duty of care to help people in need. That's what I'm doing with you, Kristin."

She felt her back press up against a wall. He had tracked her to the end of the corridor. She felt the urge to strike out and bat him away, but for some reason, her wrists were locked to her sides. He leaned forwards until his lips were brushing her right ear. A deceitful smile spread across his lips as he whispered.

"Wake up."

TWENTY TWO

There was a bright light in her face as the car squealed into the car park, but Chantel was too disorientated from the excessive driving to see what it was. She virtually rolled out of the car onto the floor, desperately trying not to throw up.

"You know, I've leapt from the top of the Eiffel Tower with just a flag for a parachute, and I've been in a jumbo jet that crashed. But your driving…"

Frank ignored the comment, and slammed his door shut. He looked around surveying the area. The security lights were still on along with the floodlights, but no guards were there. In fact, his was the only car in the whole facility.

"Where is everybody?" he asked nobody in particular.

Chantel had regained her composure, and joined him. That was a valid question. If she had to guess, she would've said nobody had been inside this facility for at least six months. Dust from the road was mounted up against the wire fencing, moss had started to grow around the security barriers, and weeds were poking up through the tarmac.

"Why do I get the feeling I should have stayed in Wealdstone?"

Frank was actually thinking something along the same lines. His life had gotten exceptionally more complicated since the request for Kristin's release arrived on his desk. That was without the re-emergence of H. J. Enterprises. Chantel was still clinging to her files, and trying to read them as they slowly moved towards the main entrance.

"Hey, Frank? Why did this Doctor Verne keep being allowed off the hook? He had multiple counts of patient neglect, breaking licensing agreements, gross negligence and more."

Frank snorted.

"Money, Dr Beaufoy. A whole bunch of Benjamin Franklins."

Chantel looked confused.

"I presume that's a lot? I dunno I'm used to Euros."

Frank shook his head, his hand moving to draw his pistol, preparing for the unexpected.

"Yeah, a lot. He tried to bribe me once when Kristin first got admitted. I turned him down, he got all snooty, and then ended up bribing an older detective that had a gambling problem. Pretty sure that's how she ended up here if I'm honest."

Frank used his foot to gently kick open the single paned glass door that led to the reception. The second he walked in, the smell of death washed over him, and immediately caused him to dive to the side and empty the contents of his stomach onto the floor. Within seconds, Chantel was on the opposite side of the door doing the same thing.

Frank grabbed his tie, and held it against his nose and mouth. Chantel dug into her bag and pulled out a disposable surgical mask, and slid it onto her face.

"Yeah this ain't good."

Only emergency lights were active, giving a very dim glow along the hallways ahead, but it was enough light to see that there was nobody here. Mail was piled up behind the now pushed open door. At least six months worth. Frank gestured for Chantel to stay behind him, and she duly obliged, but she wasn't your typical scientist. She lay her bag and notes down by the reception desk, reached in, and withdrew her own weapon. It was like nothing Frank had ever seen.

The gun itself was silver with a marble grip. The barrel appeared to be wider than one would expect for a pistol of its size. As he watched, Chantel loaded some kind of bullet into the chamber that mystified him. It could have been the light, but he swore it was transparent and that he saw liquid moving within it. A noise in the distance grabbed his attention, and both he and Chantel instantly raised their weapons, the latter having also activated a small LED torch attached to the top.

"Where did you get that thing?" Frank asked astonished.

Chantel smiled.

"Part of the benefit of living through a zombie apocalypse and joining a gang of paranormal investigators."

Frank really wasn't sure what to do with that, so he just nodded and continued forward into the gloomy corridor behind the reception desk. He saw masses of shattered glass all over the floor. It appeared that every window had been blown out at some point. But the real indication something was definitely wrong was pointed out to him by his companion just moments later.

"Frank?"

He turned and saw Chantel's light was pointed at the edge of a window frame. Dried blood now awash with flies and maggots bathed the wall below the frame, pooling on the floor.

"Shouldn't we wait for your backup to arrive?" she asked tentatively.

He shook his head.

"There's no time. Kristin is clearly in trouble. Mad or not, she needs our help."

They pushed on for what felt like miles. Winding through the facility step by step, cautiously, more glass crunching beneath their feet and broken tiles on both the walls and the floor. Some places seemed like it was impact damage.

Then they came to a signposted area.

"The Wealdstone Wing."

The sign was clearly handmade, and had been placed over the genuine ward number. Frank noticed the pungent aroma of rotting flesh was particularly intense here, and against his better judgement, turned into the wing.

What greeted him would live with him forever.

Two feet ahead of him, piled floor to ceiling was a mountain of dead bodies in various states of decomposition. The deafening sound of flies buzzing forced both him and Chantel to cover their ears, but neither could prevent themselves from vomiting once again. It wasn't just the sight of so many bodies. There were randomly scattered limbs amongst the sculpture of death. Objects used in the killing of some of the guards still protruded through the blood soaked and tattered uniforms adorning their corpses. Bones were clearly broken with some legs and arms bent in the opposite direction they were able to during life.

"What the fuck happened here?"

Frank's question was all he could muster in terms of speech, and despite the hideous visage that he was standing in front of, he couldn't break his gaze. Sweat began to trickle down his forehead, and he had to discard his jacket and loosen his tie. The anxiety within him was at an all time high, and his hands were now trembling, the barrel of his gun wavering.

Frank had seen his fair share of death whilst serving with the police force, but nothing on this scale. This was mass murder on the scale of a terrorist attack.

Again, Chantel was first to spot something.

"Frank! Up there!"

Her light caught the fleeting presence of something crawling along the ceiling near to the body pile. It was too fast, but she managed to keep catching the tail end of whatever it was, enough to learn its direction. Frank fired two shots, but struck the wall both times, sending concrete and tiles raining from above.

"Jesus fucking Christ, I'm in an actual nightmare."

TWENTY THREE

It took several minutes for Kristin's mind to stop spinning just enough for her to focus her vision. She was wildly confused, feeling nauseous, and her body heat was off the scale. Her entire body was slick with sweat, and she felt tightness in her chest.

"I was wondering when you were going to come back to me."

The voice penetrated her stomach like a knife. Christian Verne was sat in a chair alongside where she was strapped to the table. A quick glance to her left confirmed she was still hooked up to the IV drip containing the orange coloured serum.

"What?"

Christian giggled at her confusion.

"You do remember this room, don't you?" he asked coyly as he rose from his chair.

"But… the meeting in your office, the whole building was… I killed you!"

More deep laughter from the man to her right.

"I'm afraid that was all inside your head, Kristin. You've been here in this room with me for, oh, going on six days now. Almost a new record. And the things I've discovered about you, will keep me elevated at the top of my field for generations to come!"

Christian started pacing around the room excitedly, and rushed over to a nearby table snatching up some kind of paperwork.

"The serum has performed perfectly. You were in a lucid state for the first two days, but once I increased the dosage, you managed to become more coherent, and I saw the untapped power within you! I knew it was there!"

Kristin was becoming more frantic, but when she scanned the room around her, her eyes fell upon a familiar sight. Christian did not miss the look.

"Ah yes, my dear friend Kenrick. Not the Kenrick you know of course, oh no, that was just your mind playing tricks with you."

Kenrick's body was on the floor exactly where she remembered leaving it, but it was considerably decomposed, and it was only now that she started to smell the aroma from the corpse itself.

"What the FUCK have you done to me?!" she screamed.

Christian appeared insulted, and feigned a distressed look.

"Why, I have been working on unlocking your full potential, Kristin. You have a power within you, that with just the right balance of chemicals, can be controlled and utilised for very specific tasks."

Flashes of memory blazed across Kristin's eyes. She saw recalls of killing Christian twice, conversations with Angie, imagery from her life replayed, and experiences in the hospital that she clearly was aware of, but now she was unsure where she was. And more worryingly, *who* she was.

"How long… how long since everybody died?"

Christian shuffled through his papers nonchalantly.

"Hmm? Oh give or take a day or two, roughly six months. Well, Kenrick here was probably five months ago, but decomposition isn't really my specialty."

That was the moment she knew. Christian was insane.

"You've had a corpse lying on the floor for five months? You're a maniac."

That pushed a button.

Christian launched his papers back onto the table, and his face contorted into a monstrous rage, spittle flying everywhere, and Kristin swore she saw his muscles begin to expand under his shirt, and his neck grew wider, veins popping all along the edges.

"A MANIAC?!" he growled. "I AM A DOCTOR! I AM HELPING PEOPLE! YOU ARE THE MANIAC, MY DEAR! YOU ARE THE ONE WHO KILLED EVERY SINGLE PERSON IN THIS FACILITY… NOT ME!"

He turned away from her, and she saw his breathing gradually become shallower, and he seemed to shrink down to a more normal stature. Although what she had just witnessed disturbed her greatly, her mind was stuck on the information he had just passed on to her.

"I… I killed them?"

Christian downed a nearby glass of water, and took several deep breaths, before turning back to her, the grin returned to his face.

"What do you remember, exactly? From your waking life?"

"My waking life?"

"Talk me through the events as you believe you experienced them."

He sat himself down in the now righted chair, grabbed a notepad and pen and began scribbling away like a deranged shrink in their weekly session.

"I remember being in this room, on this table. I remember this serum of yours. It… calmed my mind. I could focus. I remember the entity attacking us. Then its somewhat of a blur, but we were in your office, the power went out, and something was out there… killing everyone."

Christian's scribblings became even more frantic.

"That's very interesting. Because that was as I say nearly six months ago, and you haven't left this room since. When I say that was six months ago, I mean the part where you were put on that table. Everything else you described… well it never happened."

The smile on his still red face grew, and Kristin could feel her heart rate increasing beyond safe levels. A pain began tearing its way through her head, all of the frightening imagery of the past gradually moving to the forefront. The serum, it appeared, was wearing off.

"No… no you're lying. That can't be right. The entity… your wife… how can I remember all that?"

Tears streamed down her face and mingled with the sweat. Christian's face did not change from his permanent grin. It was as if he could see the rage being summoned within his latest experiment.

Kristin's movements however, became more and more violent, her limbs now beginning to fray the straps holding her down. The table began to move as she threw herself left and right, and tensed every muscle in her body. Christian gradually got up from his chair and moved slowly away from her, his eyes glancing at the now empty IV bag on the trolley.

With a mighty roar, Kristin ripped the arm restraints away from the table, the leather straps clattering to the floor. She grabbed hold of the chest restraint and snapped it in two, her eyes burning with violet light. Her teeth bared and she snarled at Christian as she tore the needle from her vein, blood slowly dripping from the bruised wound.

She clenched her eyes shut trying to focus all of the anger, and rage and pain she was experiencing, but it was no use. She zoned in on Christian and leapt forward in his direction. What she didn't expect to happen was to find herself throat punched with such force by him, that she flew backwards through the air, and broke clean through the wall that was located behind her table. Bricks and plaster cascaded from the ceiling as Christian once again became the snarling beast she had seen moments before.

He stepped through the hole in the wall and leaned over Kristin.

"You see my dear, I have spent a lot of time attempting to reach the very top. To be the envy of the medical world, and unlock human potential. Then you came along."

He grabbed Kristin by the throat once more, and lifted her clean off the ground with one arm. With a sharp jerk, he threw her sideways crashing through several pieces of old medical equipment and a gurney, slamming to the floor, cracking the tiles all around her. The pain was now blinding both physically and mentally.

"I'd tracked you for years. I was suspicious of what your little group was doing. Encounters with vampires, werewolves, wraiths, and yet you were still living life to its fullest."

He swiped the broken table aside, and once again launched Kristin through the air, this time exploding through an observation window to the courtyard outside. The glass shredded her arms and small pieces protruded from her face. She tried to catch her breath and stem her sensory overload, but he didn't give her time.

"Then, when I heard about what happened to you at Crossroads, I knew you were the perfect candidate for my experiments. Unlocking hidden powers within. It's something I tried myself, with… varying results."

A swift kick to the abdomen, left Kristin rolling across the damp grass and spitting blood. She heard a voice in her head speak to her softly.

"Find me, Kristin. Don't let him take you."

Another kick to the ribs, and she was launched against the external concrete wall of the building, landing on her shoulders. The left one buckled on impact.

"You see, I was always being trodden on. The little scientist guy who always failed. Nobody could see my potential. So I created this serum. Oh not the one you've been given, a slightly milder one. I tried testing it on my step-daughter, but… she wasn't strong enough. Shame really. She was a lovely girl."

Kristin's vision suddenly became clear.

From through the broken window, she saw the familiar black and teal swirling mass making its way into the room she had just been thrown out of. The presence was close enough to help her stabilise her control, but it appeared like it was stuck in the room. Christian, unaware continued his rant.

"But when you bonded with the serum, and I started to see the anger and the strength from this pain wraith exposure come to the surface, I knew it was exactly what I needed. So I took your blood, and the serum, and injected them both into myself. AND LOOK AT ME NOW!"

He aimed his boot towards her face but Kristin launched her hand up and grabbed hold of it, stopping it in mid air. Christian's face dropped. Kristin looked up from her knees and a wry smile crept across her face.

"All I see, is a grade A asshole."

She twisted his ankle round, grabbed the back of his leg, and launched Christian as far as she could throw him. He travelled a great distance before slamming into the ground in front of the broken window. She stood up, defiant, eyes glowing, and her shoulder crunched back into alignment, the sound echoing around the empty courtyard. As she strolled towards him, the shards of glass dropped from her face and her wounds began to heal.

Christian pulled himself back to his feet, the shock clearly affecting his alter ego, which had now receded away again. As he prepared for her attack, and tried to summon his inner monster, two gunshots rang out inside. He looked over his shoulder, and dived back through the window, and vanished out of view. Kristin also noticed that the entity had gone too, and wondered if the gunshots were anything to do with its presence.

That meant they had company.

Kristin took several deep breaths, and began to calm herself. The rush of endorphins she was experiencing was at an all time high. Clearly if her memories were now hallucinations, this was not one of them. Hurting Christian had given her pleasure.

It was time to hunt him down.

TWENTY FOUR

To say that Kristin was confused would be an understatement. Moments ago, she had leapt through a broken window into the building to hunt Christian down. Now, however, she was bolt upright in her bed, back in her cell in the main hospital. There had been no gap in her memory between launching into the building and sitting bolt upright. The sun was absent, and the only light coming in from the small window was cast by the moon.

Her breathing was rapid, her body bathed in sweat, but she had no evidence of her battle with Christian, or whatever he had transformed into.

"Confusing isn't it?"

Kristin jerked her neck to the left to see the tangled web of matter slowly forming to create the familiar form of Angie.

"What… what is going on here?!" Kristin exclaimed, almost painfully so.

Angie seemed to float across to her side, and looked down at her, still nothing in the sockets where her eyes should be, but a certain degree of warmth in her presence. It was only when Angie was around, Kristin felt any kind of calm.

But not this time.

"He is closing in on you, Kristin. You can't allow him to continue. After he's done with you, he'll have unlocked a power he cannot possibly comprehend."

Kristin jumped up out of the bed and stormed to the wall opposite, before starting to pound at the tiles. When the first one cracked and fell from the wall, Kristin noticed Angie was once again next to her, despite there being no sound projected from her movements.

"Who are you? Are you really his wife? Are you really dead? Is any of this even FUCKING REAL?!?!"

Angie smiled slightly.

"You are real, Kristin. What's happening to you is real. Everything you have seen or experienced in some way is real. You're just experiencing it out of order."

That got her attention.

"What do you mean, out of order?"

Angie began to move towards the door, but this time, Kristin wanted her answers.

"NO YOU FUCKING DON'T!"

She lunged forward, but a surge of purple energy burst from her hand and blew Angie off to the side before she could reach her. Wide eyed and staring down at her hands, which were still glowing, she felt the surge of dopamine in her system and she felt the smile begin to form. When she looked up, she saw Angie was doing the same thing.

"Okay Kristin. I'll explain what's going on. But I want something from you."

Kristin felt the strongest she had felt yet, and she liked it. The feeling was encouraging her to comply. Her own thought process was becoming buried in the high of her ever developing powers.

"Name it."

Angie smiled once more and floated to Kristin's side. She moved her dead lips up to her ear, and whispered.

"Help me out of here."

A demonic lizard like tongue flicked out of Angie's mouth and grazed Kristin's earlobe twice, before retracting. Unaware of this, and still in an incredibly persuasive state, Kristin turned to face her.

"Deal."

Angie couldn't help but let out a greedy shriek of delight, but remembered her promise.

"This, is a memory. You remember this, don't you?"

A whirlwind of colours and a strong breeze blew away her room, and she was standing in the shower block, naked, in front of the stream of water.

"This was the first time I appeared to you. The first time I became aware of what you were."

Kristin was no longer self conscious of her current state and turned to face Angie.

"I remember. I felt vulnerable being in here. Just me and that pervert female guard. She used any excuse she could to ogle me. I remember being horrified at what I did to her, but now… now it makes me feel good."

Angie nodded, wisps of her hair moving almost independently from the rest of her form.

"I sensed you were different on your arrival. There was a power in you, waiting to be unlocked. I knew Henry… Christian had brought you here for a reason."

Kristin turned around, the sound of the water now irritating her on a cellular level. It made her skin goosebump, and she had no desire to remain here. The female guard approached as she had done previously.

"Hey, I said…"

Kristin, without even blinking, reached forward and grabbed the guard by the throat, lifting her off the floor. It was the same action she had used on Kenrick. At least, that's what she remembered. She held her there for a moment, and turned to Angie.

"If I kill this bitch here and now, does it change anything? Or is it simply a sandbox of memories where I can do what I want without consequences?"

Angie leaned forwards, her curiosity clearly peaked.

"It's a memory. Kill her. You know you want to. You enjoyed it once before, why not again?"

Kristin did feel aroused at the thought of how killing the guard for a second time would give her such a rush. Rather unexpectedly, however, she dropped the guard back onto her feet. She gasped for air, but the relief lasted only a couple of seconds. Kristin reached both hands up, grabbed her head and twisted sharply. The snapping of the guard's neck gave her a surge of pleasure, and her eyes closed, as if trying to savour the moment. As her body hit the floor, Kristin opened her eyes.

"How did that feel?" came the whispering voice of her companion.

"Incredible."

Kristin's face had transformed to that of a person possessed. Eyes, raging with violet light, veins and muscles tensed to their maximum.

"Tell me more."

Angie tilted her head to the side in acknowledgement of the request.

"He targeted you. He brought you here to examine you, subject you to various experiments as he had done so many times to others, and extract your power to feed his own curious scientific interests. But his need for power has grown beyond what he can harness. The slight input of your evolved DNA has created an alternate personality within him."

The scene whizzed by once more, and Kristin now saw herself strapped to the table, and Christian hunched over a desk, tightening a strap around his right arm. They watched as he picked up a needle containing what looked like blood, but there was a violet tint to the crimson, and a slight shimmer to the fluid.

"This is when it happened."

They watched as Christian injected the modified blood into his arm, and lower the syringe. For a few moments, nothing happened. But from that point, the transformation was fast and incredible. He doubled over, clutching his stomach, and a rip appeared in the back of his shirt running the length of his spine. The cuffs on his sleeves also burst as his muscles increased in both size and tensity. Even his head seemed to grow, and his skin developed a more grey hue. He let out a loud roar, spittle flying across the table in front of him, before he paused, his breathing now heavy and fast paced. He appeared to have transformed, but he spoke coherently.

"I… I did it. I feel… powerful."

He turned towards them and they saw his eyes were black, his jeans had several rips in them, but although the words were coherent, the voice did not sound like Christian. The vocal tone was far deeper, gruff, raspy in places, and with a more pronounced sound.

"I knew that we could do it."

Rather unusually, a second voice came from the same mouth that uttered the first words.

"You need to give me back control. We aren't ready for this yet."

"NO! The power is incredible. Feeling such strength!"

"We need to study it more."

"NO!"

The scene was remarkable. Two distinct personalities existing in one man, following the injection of a modified blood serum. Kristin was beginning to feel like the blanks were being filled in her story.

"When did he do this?" she asked.

"This is almost your most recent memory. The developments within you are showing you repeats of actual images and variations. By human definitions, you are indeed insane."

Kristin would have previously been offended by this, but she was simply in awe of this beast stomping around the room next to her unconscious body, arguing with himself in two different voices.

"I WILL NOT HIDE AWAY! I HAVE BEEN SET FREE!"

"You must calm yourself. We cannot risk being exposed."

The beast side of the man was however grinning.

"Hide away… Hide. I like that. You have kept me locked away all of this time, Henry. Now I am free. Perhaps an ironic name to celebrate my freedom. You may call me… Hyde."

Kristin finally broke her gaze and looked back at Angie.

"Why do you all keep calling Christian by the name of Henry? You said it was his real name. What was he before? I've seen the memories in the warehouse and the experiments on the people."

Angie looked back at the huge man who was beginning to return to normal size and stature, much to the disgust of the more violent personality.

"His real name… is Henry Jekyll. He was the CEO of H. J. Enterprises. Specialising in regenerative medicine and attempting to unlock the full potential of the human brain through… unorthodox experiments."

The scene faded away and Kristin now found herself standing on the broken shards of glass just inside the window she had been thrown through. Angie was floating opposite.

"Wait, so is this real? Is this now?" she asked frantically, some of the dopamine running low.

Angie turned towards her.

"It's real. I tried to go after him, but I am not powerful enough. I cannot leave this building. It is where I was killed. But you can. You must find him, Kristin. When he is stopped, I can leave."

Kristin's thoughts flashed back to the feeling of stamping his head into the concrete. Shooting him with his own bullets. Battling with him on the grass outside. Her veins began to burn like fire as the power within her began to return.

"Then let's get to it."

TWENTY FIVE

The smell of death was now permanently under Frank's nose. The image of the Wealdstone Wing piled high with decaying bodies would never leave. He even wondered if experiencing such a thing would lead him to become an inmate of a place like this. He was one of the many people who considered being within a facility like this as a prison with nurses. They were designed to keep the extremely mentally ill people away from the rest of society and nothing more. It sickened him that in the twenty-first century, humanity still locked away their most vulnerable instead of focussing on helping them.

"I didn't like the sound of that, Frank."

Chantel was far from cowering behind the detective, but the thunderous noises they had heard from below their feet had increased both of their levels of fear.

"Yeah, that was definitely loud, and destructive."

Chantel scoffed.

"So remind me why we are going in the direction it came from again instead of waiting for backup?"

Frank stopped and turned to her, the light on her gun blinding him briefly.

"Do you wanna help your friend or not?" he asked, impatiently.

Again, Chantel laughed off the suggestion.

"Hey, she isn't my friend. I only knew her a few hours and I saw her stab one of her best friends to death, and the official breakdown of her marriage. I'm here because she's my girlfriend's aunt. That, and I'm intrigued by Doctor Verne's research."

Frank turned back to face forwards, and increased his pace slightly. Typical squint. Surrounded by danger, but still desperate for new notes or research into possible breakthroughs. Truth be told, it was not the smashing of glass that had disturbed the two of them the most.

It was the animalistic roar which bellowed through the hallways. In fact it had had such a powerful effect, that they had almost completely forgotten about the dark shadow creature on the ceiling.

The same shadow creature which now hovered above them in the darkness looking down.

It moved, like a cat. Purposefully, stealthily, quietly. Actively tracking them from above, wisps of black and teal ribbons clutching at the decayed and broken polystyrene roofing tiles. The entity clearly had no real mass, as the tiles did not move. It was as if they were held together with static energy.

Chantel stopped.

"Do you feel that?" she asked, her eyes scanning the darkness around them, her torch following the gaze.

A gush of air flew past her quicker than her torch could match.

"Frank? What was that?"

No reply.

"Frank, you must have felt that."

Still, silence.

Chantel span on the spot several times, the beam of her bright led light illuminating each surface it touched. But it was no use.

Frank was gone.

She closed her eyes, took a deep breath, and counted.

"Un, deux, trois, quatre…"

A scuffling sound came from ahead of her. She continued to count, trying to calm her breathing.

"Cinq, six, sept, huit, neuf…"

More scuffling close by. She raised her gun, still with eyes closed, took another deep breath…

"Dix."

She threw open her eyes and unloaded her weapon five times. The figure tried to dart out of the way, but the sound of bullets penetrating skin and the blood spattering on the wall could be heard. Although she couldn't see what or who she had hit, it was obvious it was a person. A broad shoulder barged her aside, and she fell to the floor, her gun clattering away from her, spinning to illuminate her own face and nothing more. The footsteps disappeared into the distance.

Trying to shield her eyes from the light, she crawled forward, and her hand became immersed in a sticky liquid.

"Oh my God," she cried out.

Grabbing the gun and light with her free hand, she aimed the light at her palm, only to see a deep red trickling down from her hand.

Blood.

She wiped her hand frantically on the leg of her jeans, but despite the removal of the blood, she still felt unclean, and her mind began to scramble. She was still seeing spots of light in her eyes from the torch, which was affecting her ability to focus. She kept thinking of how simple life had been before the apocalypse in her own reality. Even that was seemingly straight forward compared to what she had experienced since she arrived in Wealdstone. She was a scientist. That is what she loved, and it is what she always wanted to do. Now she was some kind of scientist hunter hybrid, and the early stages of such a role were taking their toll on her. She now understood why Grace was such a broken individual.

After a few moments, she managed to slow her breathing long enough to allow the sunspots in her eyes to dissipate. Without Frank, she was on her own. It had occurred to her that she may have shot him, and that he had been the person barging through. She quickly banished that thought, however, when she decided he would certainly have had something to say about it.

Finally, she reached the end of the corridor and arrived at a set of stairs which descended down into the final level of the hospital. Things were different here. The atmosphere was darker, the air felt thicker, and she felt like there were eyes everywhere.

BANG!

A gunshot from below.

BANG!

A second shot rang out.

BANG!

The third shot was accompanied by a scream. A man's scream.

Frank's scream.

Without hesitation, Chantel leapt up onto the smooth banister railing, and slid down the staircase with speed, her weapon trained directly ahead at a forty-five degree angle. The weapons training that Grace had put her through in Paris was as engrained in her as any of her qualifications in science. At the base of the stairs, she hopped off the railing and her feet landed solidly, planting on the concrete tiled floor, and automatically dropping to one knee to survey both directions quickly.

And then, her torch died.

"Not now, for the love of all that is holy, not now!"

She gave the torch a whack several times, and it flickered briefly, but died all the same.

"I miss the days before damn USB charged things," she muttered as she removed the light and slipped it into her pocket.

The hallway was cast with thick, impenetrable shadows. The now weak moonlight slipped in through the frosted windows at the far end. Soon though, it lost its battle with the darkness. As if something was stood in that darkness, batting it away with its monstrous claw. Chantel looked into the darkness, waiting for her eyes to adjust, and it almost felt like it was looking back at her.

The shadows seemed to undulate as if pulsing to the beat of her heart. The pulsing increased.

Thump.

Thump.

Thump.

Thump, thump.

Thump, thump, thump.

Chantel shook her head.

"Get a grip, woman. Nothing is moving. Including you."

She spoke out loud to reassure herself, but it didn't work. There was no echo. The darkness absorbed the sound of her own voice. She waited a few more seconds, and then turned away to face down the other direction, peering as hard as she could looking for any signs of movement down there.

In the darkness behind her, Kristin watched her. Smiling.

TWENTY SIX

The sweat dripping into his eyes, made it very hard to focus on the needle's direction, and twice Christian almost stuck the tip directly into the wound. Something within him was urging him to simply stick his bare fingers into the hole and yank the bullets out, but he had so far resisted. The mental image of doing such a thing had caused him to vomit onto the already stained floor of his office. He vaguely remembered barging past whoever fired at him, but the details were vague. It was taking all of his concentration to retain his sanity.

He had turned into Hyde twice since injecting himself with Kristin's blood based serum. Both times he had remained in the background as a spectator, but as if behind bars with no real power until the effects wore off. It was those effects that he had not been prepared for, or anticipated during his long self-imposed exile at Moriarty. He could only describe it as withdrawal symptoms, similar to those of an addict attempting to go cold turkey without proper treatment, or a plan.

The experience left him almost impervious to the pain as the sharp tip of the needle pierced his skin and emerged on the other side. He pulled the thread and the skin stretched across the void to cover the hole. Alongside him on his desk were three bullets, each pulled from the wound. He had only one left to extract, the fifth having struck the wall beside him. That impact had led to a shrapnel wound on his face from broken tiles, but that one would have to wait.

As he snipped off the thread, he lowered the needle, and grabbed the tweezers. Suddenly, a flare erupted in his mind, and the more intense personality of Hyde attempted to come forward.

"Do it, Henry. Rip the bullet out with your bare hands. You know it's faster. You know you like the taste of relief after the pain. Do it!"

Christian slammed his fist on the desk.

"NO! Leave me alone, Hyde!"

Laughter inside his own head threw his aim off, and the sharp tips of the tweezers stabbed into open flesh, and he winced, cried out in pain and launched the instrument across the room.

Tears began to flow and they mixed with the equally salty beads of sweat, splashing down all over the desk. Christian was now a truly broken man.

"What have I done?" he sobbed into his folded arms, the heat radiating from him onto the wood of the desk.

"You did what you planned to do, Henry."

"Stop calling me Henry! That isn't who I am anymore!"

"Oh, but it is, Henry. You can change your name, but you can't change who you are. You have conducted your devious little experiments on innocents for decades. Don't tell me you have cold feet now?"

"It was all for the greater good of mankind, to push us further, to see just how much potential we could unlock!"

More laughter inside his head, each bellow causing pain in his temples, his muscles contracting tightly.

"Greater good. Ha! You've only ever had your greater good at heart, Henry. That is why you had to close your operation in Wealdstone. That is why you had to change your name. That

is why you were willing to experiment on young girls and maniacs to get the results you required. You're as much of a monster as I am!"

"NOOOOOOO!"

Christian leapt from the desk, grabbed the front edge, and hauled it upwards with such force that the entire solid mahogany structure lifted from the ground and flew through the window, the distant sound of the wood shattering on the pavement below echoing back up into the room.

"Ha ha ha ha. You see Henry, you can't control it. You meddled in things you couldn't even begin to realise the power of. This Kristin girl is unlike anything you have ever encountered before."

Christian shook his head from side to side, attempting to clear his mind of this insidious being he had created. Hyde was correct. He had not fully appreciated just how powerful Kristin was. His original intention had been to examine her and observe her. To see if any of the changes he had heard about were true. The higher levels of strength, the incredible mental acuity. The violence. It took him a long time to realise she wasn't a sleeper agent sent to flush him out. But as soon as he realised that her advancements were the real deal, he began the experiments in earnest.

The serum that had failed on so many others, bonded with her DNA and began to expedite the process. Whatever was within her became free, and unlocked the potential within. However, he had not been ready for just how powerful she would become. He had always dealt strictly with the science. This was something else.

Supernatural.

He was out of his depth, and by the time he realised, it was too late. He had contaminated himself with this mixture of anger, pain and violence.

What had he unleashed on the world? All of this time and effort, and bribes in the right places. Losing his wife and step-daughter.

Lucy.

Oh the things he had done to her.

Angie had been right about him. He was not only obsessed with his work, but consumed by it. There was nothing but his work. The mental discipline was instilled during his naval training, when he met Kenrick. But his own obsessions had driven him to the brink of insanity. Ironic, really.

He was now exhibiting the features on many of those who had been admitted here. Perhaps if they were not all now dead, he would find himself amongst them.

Then again, perhaps he still would.

His mind snapped back to the realisation that he was not alone in the hospital.

"She is coming for you, Henry. And so is Kristin."

But not only them. The woman he had barged over. The one who shot him. She was here also. And another. A man. Vague visions of passing a man. Had he been screaming? He couldn't remember. But there were now multiple people here.

"I have to stop them. I have to stop them all."

"Yessssssss...."

Hyde whispered like a serpent hissing at it's prey. Christian almost felt his breath on his neck, such was the closeness of him and his alter-ego.

"Stop them all. Kill them all. Destroy them before they destroy us."

Christian nodded. Without another hesitation, he plunged his forefinger and thumb into the open flesh wound containing the last bullet. The sound of squishing and squelching filled the office as the digits wriggled around looking for the metal intruder. Blood poured down his bare arm as he did so, but gripping the foreign object, he yanked it out and slammed it upright down onto the side table located to the left of where the desk had once been.

He examined it for a moment, tilting his head from side to side like a robot.

"Interesting. Unique craftsmanship."

Christian looked at the white fluid within the transparent casing. The bullet had sunk itself into deep muscle tissue and so had not lost its shape, but the design was certainly unknown to him. He gripped the casing with his bloodied hand, and felt for a way to open it. The tip began to unscrew, and he poured the liquid onto his outstretched tongue. He spat the fluid onto the floor and returned his gaze to the casing.

"Garlic… silver… and something more."

"A powerful concoction, for powerful enemies. Not meant for us, I suspect."

"Agreed. Meant for something else. I must know more about this ammunition and the creatures it is designed to take down."

He screwed the casing back together, and slipped it into his pocket, ensuring there were no holes from his battle with Kristin, or his expanding into the alternate presence within his mind.

"We must leave, Hyde."

A long guttural laugh inside his mind burst forth.

"Yes… but first… let's tear her apart."

Christian smiled, turned and walked out of his office, his form slowly expanding once more. Hyde had returned to full strength, and Christian was now a distant prisoner.

"Come out, come out, wherever you are."

TWENTY SEVEN

Her eyes had now adjusted more to the dark, and Chantel was gradually working her way down the corridor of the ground floor. At the very end, she could see movement in a window. It looked like a tree casting a shadow on the glass, moving in the breeze. Alongside that window, was an open door. Slightly ajar, not fully open all the way. Every door in this section was closed apart from that one. There must be significance to that, she thought.

Behind her, a breeze gradually began flowing and it reached her ankles, sending a chill up her spine. Against her better judgement, she continued forwards trying to ignore whatever was behind her. As she reached the open door, she used the barrel of her gun to pull it further. Peering round the inside she saw the room was empty, but something drew her inside.

Each time she blinked, it was as if she was seeing a piece of a memory. Sunlight burnt her eyes. Then another blink, and she saw a woman being beaten. Another blink, and the woman was launched through the window. More images flashed as if she was reliving the moments. She felt the pains of the glass cutting the skin of the woman. Her head blurred as if struck in the face. She was suddenly winded, as if kicked in the ribs, and she dropped to her knees.

Then the flashes stopped and the room was silent.

"What the fuck?" she gasped out loud.

She climbed to her feet, and walked over to the window, staring out through the glass. The trees lining the rear of the hospital waved in the breeze. They almost had an enticing quality to them. Sanctuary outside of these walls. The walls of a place that seemed darker than the darkest forest. Her eyes flicked to the right at the hint of movement. Just another tree in the breeze. She returned to the centre of the tree line where she had been looking.

And someone was staring back at her.

Chantel gasped and span around, but she was held in place by Kristin's power. Her hands were outstretched, and an invisible force held Chantel's down at her side. A slight flick of the wrist, and the gun was thrown across the room. Kristin tilted her head to one side.

"Who do we have here?" she asked, a slight echo in her voice.

"Kristin?"

That was all Chantel managed to get out of her mouth before another hand gesture placed pressure on her throat, making it hard to breathe.

"How do you know me, I wonder?"

Kristin's eyes were no longer her own. Even her mannerisms were foreign to her usual ways of movement. Her head swayed from side to side as if a snake was weaving its way through long grass. Her voice was slightly higher, but surrounded Chantel when she spoke. Whatever form of transformation she had been in the grip of, now seemed complete.

Chantel's eyes began to roll back in her head as her breathing began to come to an end. Summoning all her remaining ability, she managed to utter one word.

"*Grace.*"

At the sound of that name, Kristin's smile faded and her eyes flicked left and right with such speed it appeared they were being spun in place. She recalled memory after memory of her niece. Of all the people she had been involved with, her found family included, Grace was the only one who had never hurt her in any way.

The invisible grip on Chantel evaporated, and she fell to the floor, immediately coughing and spluttering, saliva splashing against the cold floor. When she looked up, Kristin was gone.

But her horror was far from over.

Directly opposite, slumped on the floor against the door to the opposing room, was Frank. His skin clung to his bones, like damp tissue paper. His eyes were black and vacant, and a thin trail of blood was congealed at the edge of his mouth, and both ears.

Holding her mouth over her hands, and trying to come to terms with what she had just witnessed, she shakily reached for the gun, fully aware that it was unlikely to do any good against whatever creatures now inhabited this facility. But it was the only thing she had. She stood and walked slowly towards the edge of the room, took one more look at Frank's body, and turned back into the corridor.

With the first light of the morning now beginning to penetrate the darkness within the hospital, Chantel was able to catch Kristin almost floating up the stairs. But it wasn't the sight of this which stirred her blood even more than it had been.

There was a black and teal twisting mass hovering directly above her, seemingly lifting her and moving her up the stairs. She had been surprised initially to see how quickly Kristin had turned into whatever form it was that she now took. But if there really was an outside influence, speeding up the process, then she wasn't really sure what she could do. There was nobody left to call at this point. Kathryn and Jack were gone, with no idea where. Annie had returned to Montana in an effort to find a way back to Beyond, and Grace didn't even know she was here.

Her compulsion to follow Kristin was strong, and of course there was the other mysterious figure somewhere in the facility who had bashed her out of the way earlier. She suspected that this was the Doctor Christian Verne she had researched.

And then it hit her.

Research.

Her laptop and files were still in the reception of the building. She needed to know more about this institution, Kristin, any supernatural occurrences here, and any links to the doctor.

"No way am I going back through this death maze," she said to herself, and returned to the opposite end of the corridor where the broken window was, and climbed her way through to the outside.

Making her way to the perimeter fence, she felt her way along where the dawn light did not yet reach and followed it all the way around the building until she came to a locked mesh gate. Clearly this was designed to prevent patients escaping into the car park or other vital areas of the hospital.

Chantel however, was a dab hand at a lock. Reaching into her back pocket, she pulled out a manicure set, but inside was anything but dainty nail files and tweezers. In their place, were varying designs of hooks and a small tube of what looked like plasticine.

She up-ended the tube into her hand, and moulded the substance into the lock. She then placed a small length of twine, extracted from another compartment into the side of the mass, making sure it was a good inch or so into the substance, before folding it over to secure it. Chantel frantically slipped the case back into her back pocket, and from her front pocket, pulled a lighter.

She just managed to get far enough away from the gate before the lock exploded and the gate swung open. She looked at her results, and smiled.

"Science."

TWENTY EIGHT

The two of them stared at each other, one at each end of the long corridor between Christian's office, and the stairwell to the next floor. Neither one sure who would make the first move.

And he looked *different*.

Bigger.

Altered.

This was not the Christian Verne that Kristin knew.

But then again, she was not entirely Kristin anymore either. Her mind was now functioning like both a generator and a memory bank. It was as if she was now some kind of android, accessing the pain and violence in order to power her actions. Those images and experiences had now become a part of her soul. Her control was slipping away and she was becoming ruled by her mind.

As she examined her experiences in this place, she recalled the people she had killed. The guards. The nurses. Kenrick. The unknown man downstairs. Even the illusions of her killing Christian twice were part of the fuel. Those ones made her smile. But it was Christian who spoke first.

"So what now, you impressive creature?"

The voice was not Christian's. Something that he picked up on immediately.

"Oh, you were expecting the good doctor? I'm afraid not. He is… detained until further notice. I felt it necessary to take over from here."

Kristin took a gradual step forward.

"And just who might you be?" she asked coyly.

He laughed, a deep belly laugh.

"I am Hyde. I haven't chosen a first name yet. Or maybe that will be my first name. Who knows. I am the part of our doctor friend who has lain dormant for too long. The part that despite all of his errors and mistreatments and experiments and questionable choices, remained buried. You see, he had looked for a way to unlock the potential of the human brain for so long, his own mind began to deteriorate. It cost him his wife, his friends, his reputation."

The man was now becoming angrier, his words spat from his mouth with venom. He also appeared to grow slightly larger and was now the size and shape of a champion bodybuilder. Above Kristin, the twisting mass began slowly moving down from the ceiling towards her. Tendrils reached out towards her shoulder, but Kristin moved forward again, and the mass retreated slightly, its advantage gone for now.

"Then he found you, my dear. Something different. Unique. Evolving. He wanted to find out what effects his experiments would have on you. Clearly they accelerated your evolution. And when they did…"

Kristin interrupted.

"When they did, he extracted my blood, and injected it into himself. And here you are."

Hyde smiled, his teeth glistening in the morning light from the windows above.

"I am the depraved, morally free, lustful and simply evil parts of Henry, personified. And once I kill you, my dear, I will be free to continue the experiments without anything holding me back!"

Suddenly, Hyde charged down the corridor, the vibrations in the floor travelling ahead of him and rumbling under Kristin's feet. She sprinted towards him too, and as they both leapt into the air to strike their first blows, a huge bolt of purple energy shot down from the sky, smashed through the ceiling and blew the two of them apart with a shockwave so powerful, the walls in the corridor blew apart, and the ceiling above collapsed completely.

When the dust settled, a violet glow could be seen at the point with which the bolt had connected with the ground. Kristin looked up, waving away a small dust cloud.

Standing in front of her, was Ariella.

TWENTY NINE

Chantel was now stood frozen, laptop clutched in one hand, and a pile of papers scattered all over the floor.

"Not again," she said.

Behind her, she could hear sirens in the distance. The cavalry were closing in, but what had caught her attention was the intense bolt of purple lightning that she had just witnessed blow apart a section of the hospital.

Chantel had only seen Pain Wraiths at Crossroads, and still had nightmares from her brief time endowed with their powers. She had no desire to enter that compound, and whatever was going on was now beyond her.

What she had learned whilst leaning on the front of Frank's car scrambling for data, was that Christian Verne was in fact Henry Jekyll. She learned about his experiments, and his relocating on three separate occasions under different aliases.

There was also the questionable disappearance of his step-daughter Lucy. His wife Angela, had reported him for assault on the teenager on three separate occasions, and each time dropped the charges. And then when he moved into Moriarty, his name had changed, his new reputation falsified, and Lucy disappeared.

The only thing she had not yet been able to find out, is why there had been a release request lodged with the police to have Kristin freed. The company in question had been H. J. Enterprises, run by Jekyll. But he was directly involved with Kristin. Why would he have requested her release if he wanted to keep her there?

In addition, according to Frank on their drive to the facility, the doctor had appeared nervous that the request had come across. Could someone else be involved with the company that the doctor was unaware of?

Either way, she had more work to do. She climbed into the back seat of the car, flipped open the laptop once more and began typing away frantically to see just how much more dirt she could dig up before the cops arrived.

Either that, or before the world ended.

THIRTY

Hyde was still lying on his back, dazed and confused. It looked as though he was having an internal fight within his head, shaking frequently, and muttering under his breath.

Ariella did not consider him a threat, and turned her attention back to Kristin, who was now fully aware of her presence, and appeared to be staring her down, and evil smile spread from one side of her face to the other.

"Well, well, well," she began. "Look who finally decided to show up."

Ariella walked forwards, fists clenched tightly.

"Enough of this, Kristin. You need to stand down."

Kristin laughed. But the laugh was not her own. It was multiple voices.

"Where were you, Ariella, when I needed you? You told me that you were always looking down and watching us like HBO. And yet when I cry for help, you abandon me!"

Ariella stopped just feet away from Kristin.

"We had no idea what was happening to you. To bring you back into our realm would have been too dangerous. Your first experiences there have created what you are now. And you need to be stopped."

Kristin threw her hands out at her sides in protest, and her fingers began tingling with tiny violet sparks of energy.

"*I* need to be stopped? You sat on your purple cloud up there in your comfy little ethereal palace, and watched as this fucking monster tortured me, experimented on me, violated me! And you did nothing! You're just like the rest of them!"

Ariella sensed this was not going to end well, and saw the swirling mass above her friend.

"Kristin, whatever you think that thing wants with you, you're wrong! It's waiting for you to reach full power and it's going to consume you! It's not who you think it is! It's broken free from the void and now it's going to help the others find a way back! You have to trust me!"

The mass which had been presenting itself as Angie, seemed to react to her words, and lashed at Kristin's body causing her to shake her head negatively. Perhaps she was too late, but without full knowledge of just how powerful this human Pain Wraith combination was, Ariella feared she was outnumbered.

She decided that was enough talking. She launched a barrage of purple fireballs at Kristin in quick succession, but was staggered when she batted each one away with ease, her smile spreading even wider. Again she fired more energy, but again it was deflected.

"How cute. My turn."

Kristin's entire body glowed a deeper purple than Ariella, and a single, wide torrent of energy shot from the centre of her chest, Ariella diving out of the way just in time, but the blast continued on, blasted Hyde aside with force as he attempted to get back to his feet, through the end wall and into the generator room.

There was a small bang from the electrics in the room, and a small fire started near the fuel reserves. Ariella span back towards Kristin, and saw something that terrified her. As she watched, the twisting black mass reached down from the ceiling, and encompassed Kristin's body like a suit of oil. She ran towards her former friend as the substance began to vanish into her body.

"Kristin don't!" she screamed.

Ariella pulled her arm back and generated another ball of light, but before she could throw it, the newly integrated form of Kristin and Angie thrust their arm forward, and Kristin's fist plunged into Ariella's chest and out of her back.

She stopped dead, her body convulsing. Despite only assuming human form, it was the dispersion within her from Kristin's power that was causing her weakness.

"Your time has come to an end, Ariella. You, and all those who have wronged me will perish."

Kristin threw her second fist into Ariella's dwindling form and she gasped, her eyes widening until they became purple blurs. Her body began to break apart in violet strands of tissue, but was able to speak.

"Kristin… this isn't you… don't do this…"

Kristin's smile turned to pure hatred, her teeth gritted, her eyes burning and she pressed her face towards Ariella's.

"I will watch as they all burn!"

With a roar, and a swift movement, Kristin ripped her arms apart, tearing through Ariella's body and out the other side. As she watched, the energy that had once made up her friend and ally, dwindled and faded into tiny little sparkles, before dissipating entirely.

A rush of energy and power erupted throughout Kristin's body as the dark entity completed its integration with her, forcing her to drop to her knees. Her breathing intensified, and her dark purple glow began to morph and change until all traces of violet energy were gone, and replaced with black twisting ribbons of mass. Her eyes became black and withdrawn, and her lips began to crack and develop dark lines.

What was happening to her? She was unsure. This is not what she envisaged. Angie had told her that she needed Christian to be dead for her to leave. Ariella had struck him down, but was he dead? Looking around she could not see Hyde anywhere. Her mind was spinning so fast that she could not focus for more than a second.

A whooshing noise came from inside the generator room ahead. The battle had completely distracted her from the fact the fire was spreading, and it now engulfed the gas and oil canisters. Before Kristin even had time to gasp, the fireball erupted in all directions, tearing through the hospital.

Every window in the building systematically blew outwards, each wall collapsed, the ceilings caving on top of them. Within the echoes and eruptions within the explosions, there were echoes of screams of the dead. Within seconds, the entire hospital was gone, and there was nothing but a hole in the ground filled with rubble.

THIRTY ONE

The scene was far too familiar for Kristin's liking. She was instantly filled with fear and anxiety. The room was black. Completely dark, and no breeze or indication of life. She had been here before. Her time in the Realm of Screams had begun here. But this time, she wasn't in that realm. She was inside her own mind.

A small hiss came from the darkness, before a slim glow of light came from above somewhere and illuminated the twisting mass that she had known as Angie.

"Who are you?" asked Kristin, now certain she had been misled.

"I am not a who, I am 'we'."

The twisting mass snaked through the air towards her, before assembling itself into the form Kristin had been more familiar with. Angie once more stood in front of her.

"You're not his wife are you?"

The demon smiled, before it contorted and twisted. Moments later, a younger woman was standing in front Kristin. The eyes were the same, but nothing else. But something stirred in Kristin, that created a sense of familiarity despite having never seen this woman before.

"Lucy?" she asked.

The woman nodded.

"I am not human. I'm not a demon. I'm something… *more*. And now thanks to you and your abilities, I can go wherever I choose."

Kristin knew something was not quite true when Christian had told her about her disappearance. Still, it was strange to hear the truth from her won mouth.

"He killed you, didn't he?"

Lucy nodded.

"He had been injecting me with variations of his serums since I was a little girl. My mother made some thin pathetic attempt to stop him, but she was ultimately under his thumb. When she finally saw what happened in this place, she paid the ultimate price."

She looked down at the darkened floor.

"She didn't even realise I was locked in a room right next to Naomi's."

Kristin's temples began to throb with pain, and she flinched and cowered in the darkness. Lucy continued her venomous retelling.

"The funny thing was that he succeeded in what he was trying to do. He made me smarter. I was able to do things that I never showed him. I sat in my cell, and I locked and unlocked the door with my mind. I could wander the hallways at night and explore this place."

The images that Lucy was describing were now flashing before Kristin's eyes like a picture book.

"That's when I found him. A locked room in the very depths of the hospital. Even you have never seen this place. It had a table very similar to the one you and I were strapped to. Oh yes, I spent time in that room too. There was a man, early thirties, strapped to the table, blood trickling over his bare chest from multiple puncture wounds. The latest experiment."

The man Lucy was describing was now front and centre of her vision. He was bulky, high muscle density, bare chested, sweating profusely, but unconscious. She could briefly make out a file on a nearby table with a name, but was unable to read it.

"Christian came in behind me, and hit me over the back of the head. It was instant, at least. He didn't mean to kill me, so he protested to himself at night in his office as I watched from above. He buried me under the concrete in that very room. Even his lackey Kenrick wasn't trusted with such a revelation. The man was long gone. Dead, I expect."

The sight of Christian rolling Lucy's wrapped body into the hole made her nauseous beyond human limits. Had she been awake, she surely would have emptied the contents of her stomach.

"But like I said, I was more. I watched as he buried me. And then I bumped into my good old ma."

The gruesome scene in Kristin's mind was replaced by Angie standing in Christian's office.

"She had somehow become attached to Kenrick after he killed her. Her spirit travelled with him back to Moriarty when he battered the shit out of Naomi. She tried to reason with me, tell me she did her best. But she was a coward. She was beneath me. It was the first time I had ever consumed another entity. I gained all of her memories, some of which I treated you to, Kristin. I had to keep you onside of course."

A strange scenario was now depicted of her being shown those memories. It was at this point, however, Lucy became less aggressive towards her and began to try and convince her.

"You and I are the same, Kristin. We have been hurt by those we loved. I never thought I would get out of this place. I managed it once, following him home, but it drained so much of my energy that I could never repeat it."

Now Kristin understood why Christian had claimed to see her in his house. And she was beginning to understand why her evolution was so important to Lucy. She was like a battery to her.

"You needed me to become powerful enough for you to inhabit so you could leave permanently."

Lucy nodded.

"It also needed to be someone who understood me. If you had realised what I needed you for and rejected me, it would have destroyed us both. But you are like me. You were betrayed by your wife. Manipulated by your friends. You lost family members. Others treated you like a stranger. They made you suffer a thousand lifetimes of death and agony. Should they not pay for that?"

Kristin shuddered as she recalled the noises of the people dying all around the hospital.

"The other patients? All of them. What did you do?"

Lucy had almost forgotten about all of that.

"When you first realised your abilities were coming to the fore, you sent your energy around the entire facility. Everybody fell under your control momentarily. They were endowed with your powers for a few seconds. I figured if I could tap into that then I could absorb their energy without the need for us to share a consciousness and leave of my own accord."

"You sucked them dry. You killed them."

"Technically Kristin, you killed them. You marked them and I finished them off. They were better off dead anyway. That's what I tried to tell your friend from Trinity Bay. She had residual demon energy within her from her possession, but it wasn't enough to help me. She wasn't meant to die. I was sad about that one."

Another thought was triggered.

"Ariella said you had escaped the Void. What did she mean by that?"

Lucy scoffed.

"One night, some kids broke into the facility. They thought they were gonna grab a viral TikTok video by spending the night in a mental facility undetected. I scared one of them to the point of heart attack. Their parents demanded an exorcism and so they drafted in some two-bit priest. I felt myself being pulled into the darkness. Every piece of my being, being torn apart and put back together. Luckily whatever this Void is, it's weakening, and I was pulled back here before too long."

Kristin felt herself growing closer and closer to Lucy. Her words were almost hypnotic. She had felt more like a bystander during the confrontation with Ariella, but in truth, felt no pain at killing her. It had been a true demonstration of her power, to be able to kill a Pain Wraith with her bare hands. The previous influences of Lucy's presence and making her seemingly enjoy inflicting pain, was now beginning to become a part of her own personality.

"You're right. I lost everything. I have become a monster. All because of them. Because of Kathryn."

Lucy jumped on this as quickly as she could.

"Yes. Kathryn was the one who introduced you to your extended family. It was her relationship with Jack that caused you to encounter the Pain Wraiths in the first place. He took your wife back. Your sister-in-law rejected you like a discarded candy wrapper. They are the cause of all of this death and destruction."

Kristin nodded.

"Yes. I can see that now. Kathryn. She was the cause of all of this. She never loved me. She was with me for convenience. An *experiment*. It's all because of her!"

The room around them shook violently. Kristin clenched her fists and stood to full height. A black swirl began to move around both her and Lucy, who was now smiling.

"We can take them all down, Kristin. Everyone who has ever wronged us, all of them! Nobody will ever cause us pain again!"

Kristin smiled back at Lucy, and the two forms flew together like bullets fired from a gun, and there was a bright flash of light.

When Kristin opened her eyes, she was looking up at a cloudy sky. Her fingers felt the grass beneath her hands, and she realised she was outside. Slowly, she pulled herself up to sit upright, and her eyes landed on the carnage below her. She was sat on a small hill around a hundred yards from the hospital. The fire was still in the process of being extinguished. The cars in the car park had been crushed by the flying debris, and she could just make out Chantel being loaded into the back of an ambulance. However, there was no sign of Hyde or his cowardly alter ego.

In her mind, a soft voice spoke into her ear.

"I think perhaps, we should go and find a nice place to settle down before we get to work."

Kristin nodded.

"I know just the place."

EPILOGUE

The phones had not stopped ringing all morning. For a place without a specific police jurisdiction, Trinity Bay had suddenly become a hotbed of enquiries from the local press about the activities of Frank Short.

Beth had tried to deflect as many as she possibly could, but had now just taken to ignoring them. Her cell phone rang, and a familiar number flashed up. Making an excuse, she left the office and wandered outside onto the balcony at the rear of the station. It had a beautiful view. The new building had been constructed on the sea front, and she had a clear view out into the ocean. But now was not the time to dwell on aesthetics.

"Hello?"

"Well you didn't do a very good job there, did you Beth?"

Beth let out a troubled sigh. Her hands trembled slightly.

"I didn't realise that Jekyll was gonna go completely mad. I wasn't aware he had made... advancements to his research."

The sound of lips parting on a cigarette could be heard on the line.

"I told you to get Kristin to me. I gave you the highest clearance possible to get that release authorised, and you pissed it up the wall by giving it to your old partner. Now we don't know where she is!"

"Frank was one of the few people I trusted with my life. I figured he was a safe bet. It's not like I haven't had anything happening here, you know."

"Your personal problems are not my concern. Now I'm going to have to start again. H.J. Enterprises is too tainted to assimilate into my operation. I want these advanced people rounded up as soon as possible. No excuses. Wherever they are, find them. Or I will find you. And your father will die."

The phone clicked off, and Beth was left standing there, tears forming in her eyes.

How could she do what had been asked of her, without risking everything she had? She had been put in an impossible situation, and she had to find a way out of it.

And then a spark of realisation. A contact she had only been made aware of in the last year or so. She flicked through her phonebook hoping she had not deleted the number.

There it was!

She pushed 'call' and waited anxiously for the voice on the other end of the phone. She didn't have to wait long.

"Hello?"

"Hey, it's me. I need help. Badly."

"How bad is it? You sound traumatised."

A brief pause as she looked out to sea.

"It's bad. They've got dad. And they want more."

A longer pause on the other end made her wonder if they'd put the phone down.

"I'll be there by tomorrow morning."

Beth let out a long relieved sigh.

"Thanks Grace, I owe you one."

"Technically, you owe me two at this point. Chantel is gonna be fine. But I don't fully trust you after that shit you pulled with Kristin."

Another sigh.

"I know… but I had no choice. They're gonna kill him."

"Like I said, I'll be there tomorrow morning."

Another click as the phone went dead once more. Whoever was doing this to her, whatever reason they had for it, this was far from over. Beth was about to go from being a player on the side-lines, to joining the main line-up.

AFTERWORD

Are we still here?

Did you make it through the ending?

Oh good, I was worried I may have scared you all away.

I did warn you at the very start of this book, and even in the month leading up to the book's release that this was going to be one of the darkest entries in the series to date, and I think I delivered that with a hammer blow.

So let's talk about it!

The decision to evolve Kristin's character arc into one of a villain was made a long time ago. I began to plant the seeds with the distance emerging between her and Kathryn, but even before then way back in the first Sapphire Serpent story in the first Dark Corner book, I sprinkled the fact that she was slightly devious, and willing to do sketchy shit to achieve a goal. After all you don't go from financial advisor, to one of the richest women in America by being a good girl.

But at the time, that was more of a character trait than a path. I knew that Kristin was going to evolve and become a huge threat to everyone in the series, I simply needed a way to get there, and I chose Wealdstone Crossroads as the way to do that.

There is no way that somebody can experience a thousand lifetimes of death and torture and suffering and then come out of it unchanged. But the true turning point for me was when I had Ariella explain in that book that humans were never meant to experience the level of pain the wraiths go through. That was when I realised I had an opening for the character arc I had wanted from the beginning.

I knew it had to be visceral. I have said on many, many occasions that Kristin has always been my favourite character. That means I owe her one hell of a storyline. And with my decision to bring this first phase of the series to an end at 8 books, I knew I needed to accelerate that process somewhat.

Another choice was to bring an end to Ariella's character. Much in the same way I dispatched the original Daniella off screen in Wealdstone to prove how strong Jasmine was, I wanted to do something similar here. However, I also wanted to make the point that the Pain Wraith involvement in the series ends with Phase 1, and the only way to do that was to insinuate their destruction. It also sets up a nice little conflict down the road between Kristin and Annie, so there's always that.

I focussed my previous entries much more on the action and character development side of things, particularly in Wealdstone Crossroads, so I decided to veer off the path completely for Frame of Mind. This is so far away from Crossroads, that you may be forgiven for thinking it was written by a different author. But this is what I always aspired to write. Dark horror.

There will be more to come. The books that will feature in Phase 2 are going to be more standalone but with an over-arching theme. Much more of this dark variety, but keeping the variations between shorter and longer form novels.

Frame of Mind is the shortest book in the series, and was such a dominant force in my brain, that I wrote it within three weeks. Wealdstone : Crossroads released on March

27th 2023, and Frame of Mind released 12th June 2023, so you can see how quickly the whole thing was fleshed out.

The speed came from the unprecedented support that I discovered when I opened up my literary world to TikTok, more specifically the BookTok community. I began doing daily livestreams, where people could buy the books, and interact with me and ask any questions, and it was so successful that I have found a new group of friends. This is why Frame of Mind's dedication was so widespread. These amazing people have given me newfound faith and desire in my writing, and I just want to keep going and going. They even have characters named after them throughout the series, and if they don't yet, they will do by the end of Phase 1.

Speaking of which, let's talk about Chantel!

Originally, she was going to just be a cameo towards the end, but it naturally evolved into a huge part of the secondary story. We will be seeing a lot more of her in future books throughout Phase 2, and she will evolve much more from a scientist, to a badass. I think that started pretty well in this story. I chose to set this story a year after Crossroads because I wanted things to have happened since then across the board. Chantel is obviously now one of the gang, weapons trained, alert. Combined with her experiences in the alternate Paris and at Crossroads itself, she's much more of an action hero. She will never lose that scientist element though, and that particular focus will come into play in a huge, massive way later in the series. It's a hell of a storyline, I promise you. Want a hint? Go back and look at the doctorates that I listed she has and what she's been learning. You might figure it out. But I doubt it.

Originally, the idea was for this book to be a standalone, with enough detail that you wouldn't need to read the first five books. However, given the shortness and isolated location of the story, I realised this wouldn't be possible, and direct links were needed to make the story flow as needed. I think of the first three books in the series as the opening trilogy. They are all connected, and all integral to each other. So think of Frame of Mind, as the first in the concluding trilogy of Phase 1.

So what comes next? What are the final books of Phase 1?

Well, I said there will be more dark horror, and there will. But that is not for Phase 1. That's where phase 2 kicks in. The final two books in this phase as you will know if you watch any of my livestreams are The Land Beyond, and the third Wealdstone novel, Origins.

There will also be more sci-fi in Phase 2. I'm far from done with the Resurrection series, with a third of the sequel already written.

But of course, as I said above, the next book in the series is The Land Beyond which is my first full delve into adventure fantasy. You may have noticed that one of the names on the list on Frank's desk was Joshua Shaw. Keep that in mind for this next book.

Speaking of which...

Who would like a sneak peek at the start of that adventure?

I thought so.

Dave.

FRAME OF MIND

THE
LAND BEYOND

– SNEAK PEEK –

Please enjoy the short, but action packed Prologue from the next entry in the Dark Corner Literary Universe.

The Land Beyond is due for release in late 2023.

PROLOGUE

The snarling behind them was closing in. The low guttural growls increasing in volume, drowning out the sound of their own panting and heavy breathing. Petri looked over his shoulder, and his eyes widened. The swirl of the black smoke appeared to be picking up speed. His heartbeat was deafening as it thundered in his ears. He turned back and pushed his body as hard as he could, his feet crushing the blades of grass and flowers of the meadow, making gentle squeaks as the moisture from them was released.

Berg smacked him on the shoulder and gestured for him to run faster, but Petri simply had nothing left to give. Berg, being taller and able to take bigger strides, began to move ahead and leave Petri behind.

"Wait! Berg, don't leave me!"

His cries were not enough for Berg to look back. He could see the gates to the edge of the Fifth Kingdom ahead of him, and kept his focus on those huge stone archways.

"Wait!"

The final cry came as the swirls of black smoke encircled Petri, and lifted him off the ground as if he was a small twig. The phenomenon stopped advancing as it focussed on its prey. As Berg reached the gates, he stopped and turned back. As he watched, his friend's head and shoulders emerged from the darkness, and twisted in agony, his screams no longer audible, all of the breath squeezed from his lungs. The veins erupting on his now pale face were visible even from such distance.

A section of the smog rose from the ground, and began to widen and contort. As Berg watched on, it moulded itself into a sinister wolf-like appearance, red eyes glowing against the black of its form. Long sharp teeth emerged from what resembled a mouth, and in one fell swoop, lunged over Petri's head, twisted violently, and lurched back tearing the head from his body.

Berg felt a cold, sharp pain in his stomach. This was the first time he had experienced death. His stomach began to churn, and his heart was visibly pounding against his chest, his clothing moving with the force.

The creature, shot him a look, and then almost surveyed the area, before retreating back into a singular swirling mass, and winding its way back through the meadow and out of sight, taking Petri's remains with it.

Berg remained frozen to the spot for a few moments, before managing to relay a signal to his legs to move forward. Against his better judgment, he slowly made his way back to the sight of the atrocity, something he felt he needed to do because he saw something and needed to make sure that with everything he had just witnessed, he wasn't now imagining it.

But there it was.

An imprint of sorts was burned into the ground. A snake like winding trail was scorched through the meadow, all the way back to where they had started, far beyond the view of the naked eye. A surge of panic returned to Berg, and he turned and sprinted back towards the gates, his legs now burning like fire, his chest consumed with stabbing pains. He burst through the gates and collapsed onto the cobbled street.

A nearby family spotted Berg, and ran towards him, the father picking him up from the floor, and placing him into a seated position.

"Are you okay, my young friend?" he asked.

Berg shook his head violently left to right, attempting to catch his breath and speak his words at the same time.

"The…"

The wife had now attracted the attention of members of the King's Guard, who advised her to take her children away.

"What is it?" asked the father.

Again, Berg tried to speak.

"The… the v…"

The first of the guard knelt down beside him, and put his hand on Berg's.

"Take a deep breath, slow your breathing pace. And then tell us. What were you running from?"

Berg closed his eyes, took a deep breath, and finally managed to complete his sentence.

"The void… the void has opened."

Are you seeking support for your mental health, distress, or trauma?

Look no further! Flare Peer Support is here for you. We may not be professional counsellors, but we are a compassionate peer support group that believes in the power of connection and understanding.

Talk it Out Thursdays: Every Thursday, we host structured and activity-based sessions where you can share your thoughts and experiences in a safe and supportive environment.

Self-Care Sundays: Our relaxed Sundays are dedicated to practising self-care, having fun, and building a strong community. Join us as we create a nurturing space for relaxation and rejuvenation.

We understand that some individuals may require more personalised and regular support. That's why we offer one-to-one sessions for those who feel the need for a deeper connection.

Feeling the need for a trusted confidant? Our Key-Mentor Programme pairs you with a supportive mentor who will check up on you semi-regularly. Your mentor will be there to listen, offer guidance, and provide a private space for you to express your concerns, issues, or problems happening in your life.

You don't have to face your struggles alone. Join Flare today and become a part of a caring community that understands and supports you on your journey toward mental well-being.

Find out more about Flare at
ALLMYLINKS.COM/FLARECARES

Printed in Great Britain
by Amazon